From *Black Corridors*

I waited around for a few minutes, but Frances didn't show up so I went back to my room, turned off the light, opened the door into the hall and got into bed.

I was not sleepy and I found myself watching the door, in the darkness, with some sort of vague, nervous idea that the Bakers would be coming back to finish their search.

I was hot and restless, and after a while I raised my head from the pillow and pulled my hair away from my perspiring neck. A glimmer of white on the floor between the two beds caught my eye, and I hung my head over the edge of the mattress and stared. It looked like a handkerchief or a piece of tissue paper—and yet, somehow, I continued to stare—and could feel the stir of hair along my scalp. It was a shoe—a white hospital shoe—lying on its side. I shook the hair from my eyes—and drew in my breath sharply. There was a foot in the shoe—with a leg disappearing under the other bed.

Books by Constance & Gwenyth Little

The Grey Mist Murders (1938)
The Black-Headed Pins (1938)
The Black Gloves (1939)
Black Corridors (1940)
The Black Paw (1941)
The Black Shrouds (1941)
The Black Thumb (1942)
The Black Rustle (1943)
The Black Honeymoon (1944)
Great Black Kanba (1944)
The Black Eye (1945)
The Black Stocking (1946)
The Black Goatee (1947)
The Black Coat (1948)
The Black Piano (1948)
The Black Smith (1950)
The Black House (1950)
The Blackout (1951)
The Black Dream (1952)
The Black Curl (1953)
The Black Iris (1953)

Black Corridors

by
Constance & Gwenyth Little

The Rue Morgue Press
Boulder, Colorado

About the Littles

Although all but one of their books had "black" in the title, the 21 mysteries of Constance (1899-1980) and Gwenyth (1903-1985) Little were far from somber affairs. The two Australian-born sisters from East Orange, New Jersey, were far more interested in coaxing chuckles than inducing chills from their readers.

Indeed, after their first book, *The Grey Mist Murders*, appeared in 1938, Constance rebuked an interviewer for suggesting that their murders weren't realistic by saying, "Our murderers strangle. We have no sliced-up corpses in our books." However, as the books mounted, the Littles did go in for all sorts of gruesome murder methods—"horrible," was the way their own mother described them—which included the occasional sliced-up corpse.

But the murders were always off stage and tempered by comic scenes in which bodies and other objects, including swimming pools, were constantly disappearing and reappearing. The action took place in large old mansions, boarding houses, hospitals, hotels, or on trains or ocean liners, anywhere the Littles could gather together a large cast of eccentric characters, many of whom seemed to have escaped from a Kaufman play or a Capra movie. The typical Little heroine—each book was a stand-alone—often fell under suspicion herself and turned detective to keep the police from slapping the cuffs on. Whether she was a working woman or a spoiled little rich brat, she always spoke her mind, kept her sense of humor, and got her man, both murderer and husband. But if marriage was in the offing, it was always on her terms and the vows were taken with more than a touch of cynicism. Love was grand, but it was even grander if the husband could either pitch in with the cooking and cleaning or was wealthy enough to hire household help.

Certainly Jessie Warren, the heroine of *Black Corridors*, is one of their more inspired creations—a determined redhead who can't put three words together without resorting to sarcasm, especially when talking to her aunt or a potential beau. The action in *Black Corridors* takes place in a favorite Little setting, a hospital, where murderers prefer blondes.

The Littles wrote all their books in bed—"Chairs give one backaches," Gwenyth complained—with Constance providing detailed plot outlines while Gwenyth did the final drafts. Over the years that pattern changed somewhat but Constance always insisted that Gwen "not mess up my clues." Those clues were everywhere and the Littles made sure there were no loose ends. Seemingly irrelevant events were revealed to be of major significance in the final summation.

The Littles published their two final novels, *The Black Curl* and *The Black Iris*, in 1953, and if they missed writing after that, they were at least able to devote more time to their real passion—traveling. The two made at least three trips around the world at a time when that would have been a major expedition. For more information on the Littles and their books, see the introductions by Tom & Enid Schantz to The Rue Morgue Press editions of *The Black Gloves* and *The Black Honeymoon*.

CHAPTER ONE

A LONG, low, dark blue ambulance turned in at the gate and purred expensively up the graveled drive. I watched it slide to a stop in front of the veranda before I left the window and advanced to the bed where my aunt Isabelle lay.

"Ambulance is here," I said briefly.

"They can wait," Aunt Isabelle said comfortably. "Edith is still packing my things."

I glanced at Edith Quinn, who had been nursing my aunt for several years, and spared her a moment of pity. I knew she hated these periodic trips to the hospital. She was a woman of about forty-five, with masses of dark hair and very expressive dark eyes. Her eyes this morning were obviously cursing, while her mouth calmly inquired of Aunt Isabelle whether she wanted the red flannel bed jacket.

Aunt Isabelle, in holiday mood, doubted any need for a bed jacket, since she probably would not be well enough to sit up.

"Put it in," I said to Edith and turned back to the window. I felt thoroughly out of sorts. I had no objection to Aunt Isabelle's enjoying poor health with gusto—she'd done it for years, and it was her principal interest and her greatest source of enjoyment. Further, she had money piled up in dusty stacks and could afford it. But every time she felt the need for a sojourn in the hospital she insisted that either my sister Lenore or I should accompany her. We were required to occupy one of the guest rooms in the hospital at her expense, until she breathed her last or got bored enough to go home. Lenore and I always tossed up for it, and

I had lost three times running. I had lodged a protest with Mother, giving it as my opinion that it was downright vulgar to suck up to a relative simply because she was filthy with money. However, Mother merely looked me straight in the eye and said that money had nothing to do with it. Isabelle was her elder sister and had always been good to her. Their father had left them equal parts of a small fortune, and Isabelle had concentrated on doubling and trebling her share—and had never taken time out even to get married. As for Mother's share—it seems that when you have a husband and two daughters it is practically impossible to hang onto any sizable amount of money. We had no designs on Isabelle's fortune, Mother summed up, but it was only courteous and decent that some member of the family should keep her company when she was ill and be ready to hold her hand when she died.

I observed, with some bitterness, that I should probably be too busy with my grandchildren to run around to Aunt Isabelle's deathbed—but I knew I'd have to give in. I packed a bag in silent fury, while Lenore sat on my bed, smoking a cigarette and offering irritating suggestions for relieving the boredom that stared me in the face.

"After all," she pointed out, "there is always Michael Rand."

Aunt Isabelle had always had young doctors working on her case because she thought that they had a broader outlook. Michael Rand had been attending her for over a year—which was a record—and his outlook was as broad as the Atlantic. He didn't mind how often she went to the hospital. He said that other people took trips to Europe and that as long as you enjoyed your trip it didn't really matter where you went. He added that it was all gravy for the hospital and they needed the money.

I told Lenore what she could do with Michael and closed my suitcase with a vicious snap. She drove me to Aunt Isabelle's ornate mansion in the car and, after depositing me on the veranda, gaily urged me to have a good time and drove off before I could reply.

I watched Edith Quinn now, as she finished the packing, and knew that we were twin souls in misery. Aunt Isabelle's house was the last word in comfort and luxury, and Edith's position there as trained nurse was not a bad life—but she hated being dragged into hospital routine again.

She closed a couple of bags and said mildly, "I think that's all, Miss Daniel."

Aunt Isabelle nodded. "Then you can let them come up with the stretcher. Patrick will drive you to the hospital in the limousine—I want Jessie with me in the ambulance."

I groaned inwardly, and Edith went off, after flicking me a glance of sympathy from her dark eyes.

The orderlies presently appeared and were very careful and very gentle about getting Aunt Isabelle out of her bed—not knowing that she could walk as well as either of them. I followed along and could see various faces behind various neighboring curtains.

It was very hot in the ambulance, and I was cramped and uncomfortable and conscious of staring faces all the way. I thought resentfully that I could have been swimming—I'd had an interesting invitation to go on a swimming party—and I had to swelter in a hot ambulance instead.

Aunt Isabelle started to complain that they never used the siren when they took her to the hospital—but I fixed her up by telling her that the noise would be very bad for her.

At the hospital we ran into trouble. Aunt Isabelle's favorite room was occupied, and they tried to put her somewhere else. The ensuing storm must have roused every patient on the floor—but Aunt Isabelle refused to heed either entreaties or commands. She boiled up and down the room in her nightgown and flatly refused to get into bed.

In the end they moved the old man who had her room. They were extremely careful with him, and as far as I could see he didn't even wake up. I wondered uneasily what he would think when he came to and found himself in unfamiliar surroundings.

Aunt Isabelle was installed eventually and given her supper. I saw her through it and then went to get my own meal. I ate it in solitary gloom in the solarium at the end of the guest suite—and at an hour when I would ordinarily be finishing my afternoon tea.

I was spooning up the last of the chocolate ice cream when the door opened and Dr. Rand came in. He is a tall man, with a superb physique and very blue eyes in a tanned face. I gave him a black look and returned my attention to the ice cream.

He said, "Hello," sat down and reached for one of the cookies on my tray.

"Leave it alone," I said coldly. "It's nearly inedible, but they get around that by giving you so little that you're glad to eat swill."

"For how long is Miss Daniel honoring us this time?" he asked, ignoring my temper.

"You're the doctor," I said bitterly. "You ought to know. Why don't you discharge her?"

"I can't. She has every right to spend her vacations here if she can afford it."

"Listen," I pleaded, "can't you get her out of here before Saturday night? There's a dance on that night I simply won't miss."

"You want to go with some man, I suppose."

"Did you think," I asked acidly, "that I wanted to go with Aunt Isabelle?"

"She's better company than most of the clothes racks that beau you around. Anyway, why should I give my rival a leg up? I'd vastly prefer that you stay quietly here until I've made up my mind between you and a certain blonde."

"I'll take a nap," I said. "Wake me up when you're ready to leave so that I can say good-by."

He rose. "I'm going now," he said. "Too bad about Saturday—but I think your aunt Isabelle will be leaving at ten o'clock on Sunday morning."

"Why ten o'clock?"

"Just a hunch," he said and took himself off.

I missed him after he had gone, but that's the trouble with doctors. They're always coming or going—they're never there.

I had just started on the cookies when a maid appeared with a loaded tray, which she placed on a table at the other side of the room. She was closely followed by another maid with a second tray, and after a short interval three people came in.

They were attractive—good-looking and well-dressed. There were two men, one tall and dark, the other short, and a rather petite woman with fair hair and arresting gray eyes. They sat down and looked at the two trays and then they looked around and caught me still eating from my tray. I felt distinctly guilty. I knew they were thinking that I had taken their third tray.

I smiled self-consciously. "Lovely evening," I murmured, toying with what they certainly thought was their dinner.

One of the men smiled formally, but the other two turned back to the table and began a low-voiced conversation.

I felt quite relieved when one of the maids appeared with the third tray.

They set to then and paid no further attention to me. They kept up a steady stream of talk as they ate, but their voices were too low for me to distinguish anything. I gathered that the subject was serious and that was all.

I presently forgot all about them. I leaned back in my chair, smoking a cigarette and trying to figure out ways and means of getting Aunt Isabelle home before Saturday night. I decided at last that I'd go to the dance in any case, and if Aunt Isabelle sent for me I'd get someone to say that I was ill.

I came out of my abstraction at this point to find that one of the men at the other table was asking me if I played bridge.

I said, "Yes," in considerable surprise. My previous experience of the guest suite was that the other inmates were always too bothered about a sick relative to do more than wander around, wringing their hands.

They introduced themselves in a businesslike fashion. Trevis Baker, his brother, Gregg Baker, and Mrs. Gregg Baker, whom they called Sheila.

I identified myself as Jessie Warren, and without any further waste of time we disposed ourselves around a table and were soon playing as though we were in a bridge club.

It was not long, however, before Edith Quinn came in and told me that I was wanted. I considered telling her that I was ill, but I knew I might need it for Saturday night and decided that I'd better not overwork it.

I went along to Aunt Isabelle's room and listened to her symptoms until she fell asleep in the midst of it. I slipped out quietly then, and Edith winked at me and got out her book.

As I passed the adjoining room—the one to which the old man had been transferred—I glanced in.

He was not only awake now—but, arrayed in his little hospital nightshirt, he was out of bed and standing in front of the bureau.

CHAPTER TWO

THERE WAS no nurse in the room, so I hurried along the corridor to where the nurse on floor duty sat at her white table and told her what I had seen. She went off in a hurry, with her skirts swishing importantly, and I wended my way back to the solarium.

The Bakers were still sitting at the bridge table and had their heads together, but they stopped talking when I came in and began to shuffle the cards. I realized that the game was to be close to the chest and no idle chatter, so I slipped into my chair, pulled the blind down on my face and concentrated deeply.

We played until one-thirty, and while Trevis Baker totaled the score I relaxed sufficiently to ask them for whom they were staying.

They said it was Uncle Ames Baker and that he was in the corner room at the end of the hall.

I decided that I had better break to them my guilty knowledge that Uncle Baker had been shifted up a room and that my aunt Isabelle was now installed in his old quarters.

I said cautiously, "That's funny. I'm sure my aunt is in that corner room—and there's an elderly man in the room next to her."

"Oh no—you're mistaken, my dear," Sheila said positively. "Uncle Ames is in the corner room."

I looked at them and wondered why they should all crowd into the hospital just for an uncle. I decided that he must be very ill indeed— and yet he was strong enough to get up onto his feet and walk to the bureau.

"Is he bald," I asked, "and smallish?"

Gregg said, "Yes," and Trevis, dropping the pencil and pushing the score pad away from him, muttered, "I wish we could get a drink up here."

I persisted, "There is certainly such a man in the room next to my aunt—and the last I saw of him he was out of bed and standing in front of the bureau."

This caused a mild panic. They all jumped up, looked at one another and then dashed out of the room. I followed slowly and said to myself, "A rude bunch."

The nurse at the desk looked up as I wandered along and smiled at me. I remembered her from previous visits—her name was Frances Hoffman, and she was something of a beauty, with natural blonde hair and eyes like blue pansies.

"Why the stampede?" she asked.

I shrugged. "They heard that Uncle was out of bed, and it seemed to upset them."

"Old man Baker," Frances said. "He's a pest. Remember Olive Parsons?"

I nodded.

"She's his special at night—and ever since she came on at eleven he's been trying to get out of bed. She's asked him a hundred times what he wants—but he won't talk."

"Whatever he wants," I said, "is probably in the bureau. That's where I saw him."

She rolled her eyes. "Wasn't that something? It's a good thing I caught him before old Nosy came along and saw him. There would have been hell to pay. But how did we know he was going to bounce out of it all of a sudden? He'd been out cold for so long."

"What's the matter with him?" I asked, after vaguely identifying old Nosy in my mind as some sort of a head nurse.

"Oh, I don't know. I think he fell in the bathtub or something. Concussion maybe. Olive says he's doing all right, if only he'd stop fussing about getting up and looking for things."

I moved on down the hall to where Olive Parsons was talking to the three Bakers at the door of Uncle's room. "But you see, as soon as he became conscious he demanded to be moved," she was saying. "He said he must get into another room—and we always think it best to humor them. When they're like that it's bad for them to have anything on their minds."

I winked at Olive behind the three Baker backs and moved on. Plenty of ups and downs to a nurse's life, I thought, yawning. Either you have whining patients on your hands or their whining relatives to contend with.

I slipped into the corner room and found Edith reading a book under a shaded light, while Aunt Isabelle slept like a baby.

"You're on the night shift?" I whispered to Edith.

She nodded. "It's easier on the nerves."

"How did you get away with it?"

"I told her she should have someone reliable at night when she was asleep and couldn't see what was going on."

I laughed under my breath. "Didn't she tell you she couldn't sleep a wink?"

"Oh yes. But I told her the doctor would certainly give her a sedative."

I laughed again soundlessly and, after saying good night to Edith, tiptoed out into the hall.

A glance into the next room showed Olive Parsons sitting bolt upright on a straight chair and looking decidedly sulky, while Sheila Baker occupied the armchair and Trevis the other straight chair. Gregg was perched on a stool. The old man seemed to be asleep, and they were all perfectly quiet. I wondered what they were waiting for. I knew that Olive was waiting for morning—but the others must have had something else in mind.

I went back along the corridor and found Frances still at her table. "How about a cup of coffee?" I asked.

She shook her head. "Why didn't you ask me around eleven-thirty? I might have wangled it then."

"Something to eat?" I suggested with waning hope.

"Same thing."

"Oh well," I said, "I guess I can starve."

I went along to the guest suite and walked into the wrong bedroom first. There were two bedrooms on each side of the hall, and the solarium was at the end. I went into the first room on the right, which was obviously unoccupied, and subsequently discovered that mine was the second on the right.

The Bakers, then, must have the two rooms across the hall. I was glad that they were there—they would probably relieve the tedium immensely, since they certainly were not wringing their hands over Uncle Baker. I supposed that they were more or less in my position—except that the old man was really ill. And then he could hardly be so inconsiderate as to expect them all to stay at the hospital. Perhaps they were there to keep an eye on each other in case of undue influence.

I smiled to myself and got into bed. I liked them anyway—even if they were there to see what they could get out of the old man.

It occurred to me suddenly that I was at the hospital on very similar business—sucking up to Aunt Isabelle so that she wouldn't get mad and leave her money to someone else. I felt myself blushing in the dark and mentally argued that, after all, we were Aunt Isabelle's only close relatives and it was a pity if one of us couldn't spend a few days in the hospital to humor an old lady. But I blushed again, because I knew perfectly well that if Aunt Isabelle had no money we'd tell her to stay at home where she belonged and stop her nonsense.

I was nearly asleep when I distinctly heard someone enter the next room. It woke me completely, and I raised my head from the pillow to listen. As far as I could make out someone was quietly—almost stealthily —tearing the place apart. Drawers were pulled open and gently closed again, and once I heard the click of glass in the bathroom.

I got out of bed at last in a bit of a temper. I could see no reason for all that activity in the middle of the night—especially when the room was next to mine.

As I fumbled for my slippers I heard the intruder leave and close the door softly. I went to my own door and peered out—and saw nothing but the sweep of the dim corridor.

I went slowly back to my bed, feeling decidedly puzzled. I didn't know which of the opposite rooms belonged to which of the Bakers— but I did feel that there was something mysterious about any one of them searching an unoccupied room at two in the morning.

CHAPTER THREE

I LAY AWAKE for some time that night before I drifted, at last, into a troubled sleep. I was uneasily conscious of my door standing wide open—and I think I should have closed it if I could have locked it as well. But the doors had no locks whatever, and since it was so hot I had left mine standing wide, in order to get the cross draft.

I woke in the morning to bright sunlight and a more cheerful frame of mind. It was still hot—July at its worst—but I knew it was cooler in the hospital than it would have been at home and I decided philosophically that things could have been worse. Only I must have Saturday night—no matter what.

I finished dressing and gave myself a last satisfied glance in the mirror. My hair, I decided, looked positively auburn and was a lovely color. I wore a plain white dress—smartly cut—and reflected that white and black were the only real colors for hair like mine. White in summer and black in winter.

At this point I turned to leave and realized that my door was still wide open—and had been that way while I got dressed from scratch. I thought, "Oh well—there's nothing wrong with my figure," and went out to the solarium.

Trevis Baker stood at one of the windows, apparently staring at nothing, and four breakfast trays steamed appetizingly on three different tables. I studied Trevis' profile for a moment and, concluding that his looks were well above average, I wondered whether this hospital trip was going places after all. "But probably," I thought, "the old man will die, and then they'll all go home." After which I reproved myself for being callous, advanced into the room and said brightly, "Good morning."

Trevis turned around and said, "Good morning," with a slight bow.

"Manners too," I thought with some satisfaction. I ran my eyes over the trays and asked, "Which is which?"

He smiled. "If you can remember what you ordered last night you should be able to pick yours out."

"But I can't."

"Neither can I," he said, laughing a little. "I'm waiting for Sheila and Gregg to come and pick theirs—and you and I can toss up for what's left."

"How long are they going to be?" I asked doubtfully.

He said he didn't know but he'd go and see. He went off, and I heard him bang on the door, and there was a certain amount of talk back and forth. He came back then and said that they had ordered boiled-egg breakfasts and wanted them brought into their bedroom—presumably by Trevis himself.

I waited for him while he carried the two trays to the bedroom, and then we sat down together.

"Are you terribly worried about your uncle?" I asked after a decent interval.

"No," he said frankly. "The doctors tell us that he will pull through all right."

"Oh, I'm glad," I said mechanically and had to bite my tongue to keep from asking why they were all staying there, when the old man was not in any danger. I knew I couldn't be that nosy.

"Is your aunt very ill?" he asked politely.

I gave him a searching look, but he was buttering toast rather absentmindedly, so I said dryly, "We figure she'll live, if the hospital doesn't burn down."

Michael Rand came in just then, and although nobody had asked him to he sat down at our table. I compared him—from a standpoint of beauty—with Trevis and found him wanting. Tall as Michael was, Trevis topped him by an inch or two. Michael had nice blue eyes and healthy-looking dark hair—but Trevis had very regular features—his mustache was exactly the right size, and his medium brown hair was carefully groomed back. He had very unusual eyes too. They were a light amber color, and his lashes were very black.

Michael nodded to him and winked at me—which annoyed me.

He turned to Trevis then and said impersonally, "Your uncle has had a slight setback."

Trevis looked up sharply, and there was an expression of obvious dismay on his face. "But—I thought—" he began hesitantly.

"He was better last night," Michael said, "but he isn't so well this morning. You need not be unduly alarmed, however. These heart cases—"

"You'll do your best, won't you, Doctor?" Trevis said anxiously and seemed unaware that he had interrupted one of Michael's show-off little scientific speeches.

I wondered if Trevis were fond of Uncle Baker after all—certainly Michael's report had upset him. It was news to me, too, that Michael was on the Baker case. He must be doing well—and he was still quite young. Of course he was doing well with Aunt Isabelle—but you need more than one good customer to build up a business.

"How's my aunt this morning?" I asked.

Michael grinned at me and said, "You can have three guesses."

"Very poorly," I said promptly. "What with the trip and all."

"Right," said Michael; "but I'm going to cure her."

"Of what?"

"Hypochondriasis," said Michael, rolling it out smoothly.

"I'll bet you couldn't spell it," I said spitefully. "Anyway, you cure her of hypo whatever it is—and take away her only interest in life."

Michael appeared to think this over while he absentmindedly helped himself to my last piece of toast—but I saw it going and grabbed it back.

"Greedy pig," he said mildly.

Trevis, who appeared to have been worrying quietly to himself, now stood up and murmured, "I think I'll go and see my uncle," and hurried off.

I commenced to pump Michael about Ames Baker immediately. "Is old Mr, Baker in danger?" I asked, shaking back my hair and lighting a cigarette.

Michael gave me a very blue stare and said noncommittally, "Any sick person is in danger."

"Yes—but how bad is Mr. Baker?"

"Not so bad—and not so good."

"What's the matter with him?"

"Heart."

"I heard that it was his head," I said, remembering what Frances Hoffman had told me.

Michael said, "Did you?" and began to chew on a lump of sugar that Trevis had left on his tray.

I ground my teeth and asked, "What kind of heart?"

"The usual," said Michael, "even as you and I."

"I mean what's wrong with it?"

"If you'll wait a minute I'll run along and find out. It's probably on his chart."

I counted up to ten silently and then said, "Well, it must be pretty bad if all his relatives are staying here with him."

"There are other Bakers," said Michael. "These are merely a representative selection."

"Who selected them?"

"I dunno," said Michael and appeared to swallow a yawn.

"Are there any closer relatives?"

"No—these are the closest."

"But they wouldn't all pile in here unless they expected him to die."

"You piled in here to be with your aunt—but if she dies before she's ninety I'll eat my hat."

"You know damn well that that's entirely different."

"Well," he said with his eyes on my hair, "life is unpredictable, isn't it? Take me and my blonde problem. Sometimes I think that I can't live without her, and yet at other times—"

"Desist," I said. "We are not amused."

"Neither are we," he said sternly. "You've been trying to dig out things that you know I have no right to tell you. I merely tried to change the subject."

"Pretty feeble effort," I said, sniffing. "When I want to hear about that blonde floozy of yours I'll let you know."

"She isn't mine—yet. And she is not a floozy. Further, her head, on a day like this and on an adjacent pillow, would not look like a ball of fire."

I got up and left him. But as I pushed open the door of the guest suite and went out into the corridor I wished frantically, for the millionth time, that my hair had been any color but the bright red to which I admitted—in my more honest moments.

I went down the hall and automatically glanced in at Mr. Baker's door. Trevis was not there, and I went on a few steps to my aunt's door. I looked in and felt my eyes pop. Trevis was carefully searching her room.

CHAPTER FOUR

I ADVANCED QUIETLY and saw that Miss Zimmerman, Aunt Isabelle's morning nurse, was not in the room. Aunt Isabelle, herself, was sound asleep and snoring loudly—as she always did when she slept on her back. Later, of course, she would tell everyone within listening distance that she had not slept a wink all night.

Trevis had his back to me and was going through one of the bureau drawers. I watched him for a moment and then said casually, "Can I help you?"

I could see his back stiffen, and his busy hands became still. There was a short space of what would have been silence but for Aunt Isabelle and then he turned around.

"You might give me a hand," he said with almost perfect poise. "I hate pawing through your aunt's things. But Uncle Ames has lost something and he thinks it was left in here."

It sounded reasonable enough, even though Trevis did not appear to be the sort of person who would look through my aunt's possessions while she was asleep and her nurse out of the room—unless it were something more than a toothbrush or a pair of socks.

I advanced to his side and asked, "What is it?"

"Eh? Oh—yes. It's a wallet—a small wallet."

"A wallet!" I repeated sharply. "Did he have any money in it?"

"No, no," Trevis said and allowed himself to smile for the first time. "Just some clippings—newspaper clippings, you know. He'd hate to lose them."

I began to help him then, and after a while Miss Zimmerman came back and we all searched together.

It was quickly obvious, however, that Trevis did not trust either of us. Wherever we looked he followed close behind and did it all over again himself.

I had just removed the seat cushions from the armchair when my aunt Isabelle's voice injected itself into the proceedings. It inquired, with the most scathingly bitter sarcasm, if we would like its owner to step out of the room, so that we might have a free hand.

I ran. I figured that Miss Zimmerman could handle it, since she was being paid for it, while I was working on my own time.

Trevis followed close at my heels, and we stood outside and listened to Miss Zimmerman getting it.

The day floor nurse came along after a while. I had met her on one of my previous sojourns—a pretty girl with curly brown hair and blue eyes. Her name was Virginia Young.

She raised her eyebrows at me. "What's she sore about?"

"When my aunt gets sore," I said, "she has no reticence. She was just awakened by three people mulling around among her things and paying her no attention whatever. And she's in one of her best tempers."

She clicked her tongue and, with a glance at Trevis, said, "You had a hand in it somehow, Jessie."

"Both hands," I admitted readily, "but I didn't mean to stir her up, and I'll wear kid gloves after this when I go in there. If she raises the devil about the young man being in her room tell her it was the exterminator."

Virginia squared her shoulders and walked in, and although I could not hear what she said the row died down in about two minutes. Miss Zimmerman came out, dabbing at her eyes with a handkerchief, and I whispered to her not to be a sissy.

Trevis, who had been enjoying himself, straightened up and apologized handsomely for having started the whole thing. He added that he guessed he'd better go and see his uncle and disappeared forthwith into the next room. I sidled close to the door in an effort to hear any conversation, but as far as I could make out there was no sound whatever.

Virginia Young came out of my aunt's room and hailed me. "Go on in and butter her up, Jessie, while Miss Zimmerman gets over her weeps."

"It's too soon," I protested. "She won't be fit for buttering this side of an hour."

Virginia pushed me into the room, and I advanced slowly, while Aunt Isabelle watched me with her lips in a straight line and her black eyes flashing dangerously.

"Hello," I said brightly.

This got me exactly nowhere, so I perched gingerly on the edge of a chair and tried again. "Imagine Virginia Young being on the floor. Nice girl, isn't she?"

"Is she?" said Aunt Isabelle nastily.

"I'm sorry I woke you up," I murmured.

"What on earth do you mean?" she demanded furiously. "I have not been asleep. You can be so stupid at times—I think I'll leave my money to Lenore—she has more sense."

"Entirely up to you," I said coldly. "Perhaps you'd prefer to have Lenore stay with you."

She changed the subject, as I knew she would. "Who was that man? And what was he doing in my room?"

I explained about the Bakers and the wallet, and she interrupted me as soon as she had got the main facts, "Utter rubbish! There's no wallet here. Probably he was looking for my valuables. You're only a silly girl, Jessie, and I want to warn you against that man—he's too good-looking. That type is never to be trusted."

"Well—but I think he has money," I said innocently. "And that means something. Because if you leave your money to Lenore I shall have to make sure that I'm financially secure—even if my husband is a no-good and a bum."

"Be quiet," said Aunt Isabelle, "and watch your language. I want to think."

I sat and longed for a cigarette while she thought. After a while she said in a voice of satisfaction, "Yes—I think that would be right."

"I think so too," I said automatically and in line with my policy of always agreeing with her.

"Now what rubbish are you talking?" she snapped. "How can you know what I was thinking?"

"Well," I said, caught fairly and squarely, "I thought you meant—"

But luckily she was still churning the idea around in her head. "Now the way I see it, either you or Lenore could marry Michael."

My eyebrows climbed up into my hair, but I pulled them down again and said, "Yes, ma'am."

"But I think it had better be you. Lenore has more sense than you have and she'll be able to make her way all right—I'm sure she'll get on very well. You can marry Michael."

I said, "Oh, thank you."

She ignored me and glanced at the handsome leather traveling clock on her bedside table. "He should have been here before this. I will not have him keeping me waiting while he spends his time with people who merely think they are sick."

I stared at her and was vaguely conscious that my mouth had dropped open. She frowned at me, and I pulled myself together. "You— you're surely not going to speak to him about it?"

"Don't be absurd—of course I am. It's much better to be sensible about these things."

I said weakly, "If he refuses you'll look pretty silly, won't you?"

"No," she said, "you will. Besides, he won't refuse—he can't afford to. He needs money—all young doctors do. And he needs a wife to make him look respectable and attend to his social life—it's very important. It's extremely helpful for him to have a wealthy invalid like myself too—and he'll have none of these things if he refuses."

"Suppose I refuse?"

"Then," said Aunt Isabelle, "you'd better start looking for a job right away."

"I won't refuse," I said sunnily. I felt that Michael would refuse in no uncertain terms and I should be left in Aunt Isabelle's good graces.

"Do you love him?" she asked curiously. "I had expected more opposition from you."

"Madly," I said, relaxing comfortably into my chair.

"Well, that's a good thing. Now what, in heaven's name, is delaying Michael?"

I forgot myself and took out a cigarette and was sternly commanded to put it away again.

In the silence that followed Ames Baker appeared suddenly in the doorway. He wore his hospital shirt and was in bare feet. He looked at us vaguely, shuffled over to the bureau and began unsteadily to fumble with it.

CHAPTER FIVE

I saw that Aunt Isabelle was considering hysterics, but she abandoned the idea almost immediately—probably because she was in too much of a temper. Instead she rapped out curtly, "Get him out of here."

I moved quietly to the bureau and said, "Suppose you come back to bed, Mr. Baker."

He looked at me mistily. "I must get it, you see," he whispered. "They're all looking for it—and they'll find it soon. I must get it and hide it somewhere else."

"Where is it?" I asked.

He said vaguely, "Somewhere around here," and began to fumble at one of the drawers.

"Get him out of here or I'll scream," said Aunt Isabelle tersely.

I caught hold of his arm and urged him gently toward the door. "I'll find it," I promised him soothingly, "and I'll bring it to you right away. It's a wallet, isn't it?" But he only brushed his hand unsteadily across his eyes and did not answer.

When I got him into the hall I saw his morning nurse, Miss Cassidy, running around in a dither, and I hailed her. She came flying up and took him thankfully under her wing. "For the love of God," she moaned, "what am I going. to do with him? I went out to get his broth—and he must have been right on my heels!"

"Tie his big toe to the bedpost," I suggested and went back to Aunt Isabelle.

She was peacefully snoring on her back, so I retired and hurried along to the guest suite. The solarium was deserted, and I stretched out on a wicker chaise longue and lit a cigarette. I could hear the Bakers talking in one of their bedrooms—and they buzzed without ceasing for over an hour, while I relaxed comfortably and smoked steadily against the arid spaces that would have to be spent at Aunt Isabelle's bedside.

The Negro maids presently appeared with the luncheon trays, and the Bakers followed close on their heels.

The food, as usual, was made up of little bits and pieces—tasty enough, if you noticed them going down, but sharply lacking in bulk. It left you when you had finished with the feeling that you'd had the hors d'oeuvres and had worked up a nice appetite for the rest of it.

I realized, of course, that nearly all the guests who stayed there were so worried and upset that food was quite unimportant to them. But in my case it was different, and as I glanced around at the Bakers and saw them thoughtfully licking their lips I figured that it was different with them too. I put my cigarette out and suggested that we all go down to the coffee shop.

They looked at me, and Gregg said hopefully, "Coffee shop?"

"You can get sandwiches and coffee and pie and doughnuts," I explained. "It will keep your vitals from gnawing all the afternoon."

They stood up and asked me to lead the way, and I knew then that they were not concerned about old man Baker—they were just hungry, as I was.

The coffee shop was cluttered with doctors discussing such ailments as can afflict you between the scalp and the soles of the feet, but we closed our ears and ate steadily for about half an hour. At the end of that time Gregg sat back and sighed—and then asked, with a trace of anxiety, if the coffee shop were open at dinnertime. I broke it to him gently that it was not.

"There's only one thing to do," Gregg said as we all went out into the hall. "I'm going out to find a drugstore, and I'll get a dozen-and-a-half sandwiches—the kind they wrap in waxed paper. That'll hold us until tomorrow."

He made for the front entrance, and Sheila called after him, "Get some candy, too, Gregg—and don't forget cigarettes."

He nodded, and we got into the elevator. I glanced at Sheila as we were carried upward and wondered why she hadn't taken Trevis instead of Gregg. She was a handsome, attractive girl, and Gregg was short and stocky and not nearly as good-looking as his brother. Of course there was always Aunt Isabelle's argument that beauty was only skin-deep.

Back in the guest suite, with a long hot afternoon before me, I decided to have a sleep. I went to my room, removed my dress, stretched out on the bed and fell asleep at once.

I was forced to consciousness, against my will, by Miss Zimmerman, who worried at my shoulder gently but persistently. I opened one eye and peered at her blearily.

"Miss Daniel is asking for you."

"You're kidding," I said, opening the other eye.

"No indeed," she said seriously. "She sent me to get you—and she was most emphatic."

"That's a very delicate way of putting it," I said, heaving myself off the bed. "You run along, Miss Zimmerman, and feed her a little oil—I won't be a minute."

"Oil?" she repeated with a worried frown. But before she could tell me that the doctor had not ordered any oil I took her arm and steered her into the hall. "Come on—I'm ready now anyway."

Aunt Isabelle dismissed Miss Zimmerman when we got to her room and told me to come close to the bed.

I moved over and she said, "Do you know, there's something funny about those Bakers?"

"You don't say!" I murmured.

"They're looking for something in this room. The other son—"

"Nephew," I corrected.

"All right, nephew," she said irritably. "Anyway, he was in here, and he said that when Mr. Baker was moved something had been mislaid, and he asked to be allowed to search my room. I asked him what it was that had been mislaid, and he shuffled."

"Shuffled?"

"Yes, certainly—shuffled. You know very well what I mean. He said it was just some little thing and he was sure he could find it in a few minutes."

"Did you let him look for it?" I asked interestedly.

"No. I told him I'd think it over. But you mark my words, Jessie— it's not just some little thing—it must be more important than that or they wouldn't be making a hotel lobby out of my bedroom. Now old Mr. Baker went straight to the bureau—and I believe that's where the thing is. I want you to search it, Jessie—thoroughly. And don't leave any stones unturned."

I sighed resignedly and went over the bureau with a fine-tooth comb, but I found exactly nothing except a pair of corsets that I thought had gone out with the ark.

"Do you wear these?" I asked, holding them up. "Because if you do it's no wonder you're ill so often."

"Put them away," she snapped. "It's the only kind that is at all comfortable on me—and I'll thank you to mind your own business."

Miss Zimmerman reappeared at this point to announce that it was three o'clock and she was going off and here was Miss Gould.

Miss Gould flashed us a brilliant smile, walked in briskly and started to fix up Aunt Isabelle's bed.

Aunt Isabelle made short shrift of her. "'Get away," she said with what Miss Zimmerman would have called emphasis. "When I want you to do that I'll let you know."

Miss Gould desisted, folded her mouth in a straight line and sat bolt upright on a straight chair.

"Go out for a minute," said Aunt Isabelle, "and watch my light. I'll put it on when I want you."

Miss Gould left, with outrage obvious even in the rustle of her starched skirts, and I said, "She's mad at you now."

"Rubbish!" said Aunt Isabelle. "I'm much too ill to bother about the feelings of the nurses. It's their job to try and keep my spirits up."

"Right," I said cheerfully.

"Now," she said, settling herself comfortably, "I want you to search this room from floor to ceiling."

"Oh, listen!" I groaned in dismay. "Can't Miss Gould do it?"

"No. I don't trust the nurses, and I intend to be able to tell those Bakers truthfully that whatever they have lost is not in this room. I will not have them wandering in here at all hours and making my sickroom a clearing house for lost property. Now go on, Jessie—I have no strength to argue—and be sure you don't overlook anything."

I searched the room until I was absolutely exhausted and panting with the heat, and I found absolutely nothing that did not belong either to Aunt Isabelle or to the hospital.

I came to a halt in the middle of the room and said, "Well, there you are. Unless you want me to take up the floorboards."

She said, "That will do. Now you go and tell those Bakers to stay out of my room—there is nothing here belonging to them."

"All right," I replied, glad to get away. I made for the door, but just before I got out she stopped me.

"Wait a minute, Jessie—I nearly forgot. I have good news for you. I spoke to Michael and he said it was all right—as I knew he would. He is prepared to marry you as soon as the proper arrangements can be made."

CHAPTER SIX

I WALKED SLOWLY back into the room and said politely, "I beg your pardon?"

"You heard me," she said defiantly.

"Are you telling me that Michael has agreed to marry me?"

"As soon as it could be arranged, was how he put it."

"Aunt Isabelle," I said softly, "do you really want me to marry a fortune hunter?"

She gave me a sharp look and said, "Most people who have no fortunes are hunting them, whether they admit it or not. Now Michael admitted frankly that he was interested in a blonde—but under the circumstances he was willing to give her up. You're a lucky girl, Jessie."

"Why?" I asked absently and looking at her with a troubled eye. I had felt her interfering hand in my affairs before.

"Because you have me to manage things for you when you obviously can't do it yourself," she snapped.

I stood up. "Well—good-by. I'll go and tell the Bakers to stay out of your room."

"He's buying you a ring," she called after me. "I gave him a check to get it with."

I fled. I knew there was going to be a struggle between us and I wanted time. Meanwhile, I relieved my feelings by calling Michael all kinds of a skunk.

I went straight to my room, stretched out on the bed and smoked six cigarettes in a row. I suppose that Michael thought he was being funny—but it wouldn't be so funny for me if my new escort for the dance on Saturday got to hear of it. I fell asleep at last, thinking of the utter beauty of Bill Saturday. That he was a bit of a fool I could not deny to myself—but he was beautiful—much more beautiful than Michael.

When I woke up the sun was low, and a glance at the clock showed me that it was a quarter past six. I got up and washed in a hurry. I knew my bird's food would be sitting out in the solarium and getting cold— or warm, as the case might be.

I dashed out to find all four of the trays and not a Baker in sight, so I stepped to the Gregg Bakers' door and rapped smartly. A muffled buzz of conversation stopped abruptly, and after a moment Sheila called, "Yes?"

I explained about the trays and she said, "Thank you," and they came out almost immediately.

Trevis smiled at me and said, "Sorry, we didn't hear the gong."

"I couldn't ring it," I said, "because they're using it in the ambulance."

Gregg gave me a blank stare that made me blush for my wit.

"How's your uncle this evening?" I asked after we were all seated.

"Not so well," Gregg replied. "I suppose he's holding his own but—"

"Oh, I think he'll be all right," Trevis cut in quickly. "They say we're due for a heat wave," he added with an abrupt change of subject.

I wondered why he didn't want to talk about Uncle Baker and, still puzzling over it, I murmured, "How odd."

Sheila said, "It's July. What's so odd about a heat wave?"

"Sarcasm," said Gregg shortly.

I came out of my abstraction and protested, "Oh, no—I—"

Trevis smiled at me. "You were thinking about something else, which is what any remark about the weather deserves."

I smiled back at him and decided that I liked him much better than his brother. But Sheila struck me as being a sour plum—and perhaps that accounted for Gregg's manner.

I suggested a game of bridge, but they seemed a bit reluctant. Sheila said that they had to go and see Uncle Baker, and Trevis studied the end of his cigarette in silence.

Gregg spoke up suddenly, "It won't take all night to look in on Uncle Ames. We'll be very glad to play bridge."

I had an idea that the other two were faintly surprised—but they agreed at once, and we all went down the corridor to do our various duties by our relatives.

At the desk Frances Hoffman had just come on and Virginia Young was talking to her. They waved to me and gave Trevis a couple of fancy smiles. The Gregg Bakers were more or less ignored—which did not matter because they never noticed the nurses anyway.

As we approached Uncle Baker's room I remembered Aunt Isabelle's message and handed it on—garnished up with tact and courtesy. "I really made a very thorough search," I told them, "and I'm sure the wallet—or whatever it was your uncle lost—is not in her room."

"That's very kind of you," Trevis said. "Thank you. "

"Has it been found?" I asked.

He shook his head. "Not yet."

I opened my mouth to do a little snooping, but he turned in at the door of his uncle's room, said, "See you later," and disappeared.

I shrugged and sauntered on to Aunt Isabelle.

She received me coldly. "What's the use of my having you here if I never see you? Where have you been?"

"I'm sorry," I said. "I fell asleep. Why didn't you send Miss Gould after me?"

I knew that she would have done just that if she had really wanted me—and she knew it too. But it isn't easy to have the last word with Aunt Isabelle. She said without the faintest show of self-consciousness, "I was so ill that she could not leave me."

Sheer curiosity sent my eyes to Miss Gould's face, and I saw that she was making the mistake of allowing her feelings to show very plainly upon it. Aunt Isabelle followed my glance—and there was an immediate and lively row. Miss Gould nearly got fired, but when she dissolved at last into tears Aunt Isabelle told her to stop sniveling and blow her nose—and she could stay on if she'd behave herself. She added a command to get out of the room until she dried off.

Miss Gould retired in a fury, and I started a long dribble of gossip about the Bakers, in an effort to keep Aunt Isabelle's mind and tongue away from Michael. She listened with interest until I ran out of the

Bakers and started to tell her about Bill Saturday—because I couldn't think of anything else. She fell asleep right in the middle of Bill and began her abominable snores.

I crept out of the room and found Miss Gould standing aimlessly outside the door. "Your turn," I whispered, "and don't take her temper so seriously. It's merely one of her hobbies."

Miss Gould gave me a gloomy stare and slid into the room.

I hurried along to the solarium and found the Bakers waiting for me with cards, scoring pads and tapping feet.

I remembered that there was no nonsense about the Baker bridge, so I slipped into the fourth seat, set my mouth in a straight line and sternly checked any inclination toward irrelevant remarks.

We had been playing for some time before it dawned on me that each one of them invariably took advantage of a dummy hand to slip out of the room and had always to be called back when the hand was over.

I began covertly to watch them, and the next time Trevis was dummy I caught a glimpse of him through the partly closed door. He was making straight for my bedroom.

So they were still searching for the wallet—and were now doing my room, when they knew that I would not be there. I realized that it must have been Gregg's brilliant idea and it had hit him after I'd asked them to play bridge earlier in the evening.

The next time I was dummy I left the solarium and went to my bedroom. I pulled a large square of cardboard out of the wastebasket, wrote on it, "Don't forget to look under the mattress," and displayed it prominently.

Sheila was dummy for the next hand, and I noticed that she came back without having to be called. Her face was a bright glowing pink.

She must have communicated with the other two by some sort of shin kicking, because they did not go out again, and the game proceeded peacefully until we broke up at about twelve-thirty.

I went straight to my room and found my sign still in place. "Pretending," I reflected, "that of course they never saw it, because they were never in my room."

I wondered, while I slowly undressed, what that wallet could possibly contain to throw them all into such a dither. I supposed it must be money—and a lot of money—and either it had been stolen or carried away by accident. In any case, it seemed a little pointed to search my room for the thing.

I got into a wrapper and slippers and went out into the hall to see if Frances could wangle me something to eat.

Frances was not in sight, and lights were popping all up and down the hall, outside the patients' rooms.

I supposed that she was in one of the rooms—if she wasn't talking on the telephone with her boyfriend. I knew he worked in a nightclub as a singer. I'd heard him once or twice, and though I hadn't confided in Frances to that extent—I thought he was pretty terrible.

I wandered around to the phone booths, but she wasn't there, and I thought that she must be having trouble with one of the patients. I was pretty hungry, but I finally decided against going down the hall to see if Edith could fix me up. Aunt Isabelle might be awake and she was usually in rare form, conversationally, if she were awake at night.

I waited around for a few minutes, but Frances didn't show up so I went back to my room, turned off the light, opened the door into the hall and got into bed.

I was not sleepy and I found myself watching the door, in the darkness, with some sort of vague, nervous idea that the Bakers would be coming back to finish their search.

I was hot and restless, and after a while I raised my head from the pillow and pulled my hair away from my perspiring neck. A glimmer of white on the floor between the two beds caught my eye, and I hung my head over the edge of the mattress and stared. It looked like a handkerchief or a piece of tissue paper—and yet, somehow, I continued to stare—and could feel the stir of hair along my scalp. It was a shoe—a white hospital shoe—lying on its side. I shook the hair from my eyes—and drew in my breath sharply. There was a foot in the shoe—with a leg disappearing under the other bed.

CHAPTER SEVEN

I FLUNG MYSELF out of bed and out of the room and flew through the door of the guest suite out into the main hall. It was very quiet there, and the lights looked cheerful and prosaic. I stopped at the desk to ease my labored breathing and realized, with returning self-consciousness, that my feet were bare and that I wore only a satin nightgown that I had purchased mainly for its beauty and in case of fire in the middle of the night.

Frances was nowhere in sight, and the hall was deserted. I stood by the desk for a few minutes, trying to keep my teeth from chattering, and I was just about to go and get Edith when the elevator slid into sight and Michael got out.

For once I was glad to see him. I pattered over, caught at his arm and gasped, "For God's sake, come and see what's in my room!"

He looked me over—from head to foot. "I've seen many a night-gown in my day—all in the way of business, of course—but that's the most cleverly indecent piece. Look, Jessie—your aunt would not approve. We're not married yet—and there's many a slip. You go on back to bed, and if it's a mouse I'll see that you get an exterminator in the morning."

My teeth started banging together again, and I said wildly, "Will you shut up and listen? It's under the bed—and I think it—may be Frances."

He gave me an odd look, in which there was something faintly professional, and said lightly, "Lead on. You seem to be speaking gibberish, but I'll investigate if your heart is set on it."

I made for the guest suite, and he followed. "It's a relief to me," he said chattily, "to see that you wear ivory satin nightgowns. Pink would be terrible with your hair."

But I hardly heard him. I switched on the light in my room and pointed a shaking finger at the beds. "Underneath," I whispered and saw Michael kneel down and peer under.

He raised his head again almost immediately, and when he spoke his voice had changed completely. "It's Frances," he said. "Go and get a nurse."

I stood and clung to the door with clammy, perspiring fingers while he dragged the body out.

The limp golden head was smeared and clotted with blood, and I closed my eyes for a minute while Michael raised her in his arms and laid her gently on the bed.

He bent over her—but I had caught a glimpse of her face—and I knew. She was dead.

Michael straightened up. "Didn't I tell you to go and get a nurse?"

I said, "She's dead, isn't she?" and found that I was crying.

He took my wrapper from a chair and put it on me and said in an abstracted way, "Where are your slippers?"

I stumbled around the end of the bed and found them—but he had to kneel down in the end and steer my feet into them, because I couldn't seem to do anything but kick them around. He led me out of the room then and closed the door firmly behind us.

"Can you wait here?" he asked. "And see that nobody goes in. I'll telephone downstairs from the switchboard—I shan't be a minute."

I nodded and watched him disappear through the door into the main hall. It was very quiet after he had gone, and I kept my eyes resolutely away from the black cavern of the solarium. The sound of a step in Trevis' room brought me out into a cold perspiration, and a moment later his door opened and he looked out. "What's going on?" he asked, staring at me.

I drew a short breath of relief. "I don't know exactly. Something terrible has happened to Frances."

"Who's Frances?"

"The nurse—on this floor at night."

The door from the main hall was pushed open abruptly, and Michael came in with Edith. They ignored me completely and went into my room together. I stayed outside, because I did not want to look at Frances' pretty, still face again—but Trevis crossed the hall and peered in at the door.

Several nurses came in after a while and two orderlies, and I could hear the stir of feet and the murmur of voices from my room. I felt that I could not stand up any longer, and when Edith Quinn moved close to the door I caught her arm and whispered that she'd have to get me some coffee.

She came out into the hall and looked me over rather coldly. "All right," she said resignedly. "I know my place. The boss's niece wants coffee, so I'll have to go and get it—and miss everything that's going on."

"I'll keep a diary for you while you're gone," I said. "Don't be a pill, Edith. I'm going to cave in if I don't get some coffee."

Trevis turned on the charm and said, "May I have some too?"

That settled it, of course. Her face relaxed into a silly smile, and she went off without further ado.

Trevis and I hung around in the hall. We saw some of the nurses go away, and after a while some men came in—a policeman in uniform and two men in plain clothes.

"Why are they here?" I whispered to Trevis, but he only shook his head with a faint frown.

Edith came back with the coffee, and we took it into the solarium. She gave Trevis a nice smile and then went off and tried to get back into my room—but I think the bluecoat barred the way firmly.

I told Trevis the whole story while we drank our coffee. I had an uneasy feeling that I should be keeping it to myself—but no one else seemed to want to hear it—and I had to tell somebody or break wide open.

Michael came in after a while and said, "Come on, Jessie—they want to question you."

I went with him and whispered on the way, "What's the matter? Wasn't it an accident?"

"Don't see how it could have been," he said gravely. "Head was smashed like an eggshell. She couldn't have done it by falling—and in any case, she couldn't have fallen into that position under the bed."

"You mean somebody hit her?"

"Looks like it."

He ushered me into my room, and I came face to face with the two men in plain clothes. One was tall and the other short. The short one did all the talking.

He questioned me closely about the entire evening, and I told him everything, except about the Bakers having searched my room. I did not want to get them into unnecessary trouble and I felt sure that it had nothing to do with poor Frances.

My conscience bothered me a little, however, and it wasn't long before I bitterly regretted my noble impulse.

The short man suddenly produced—like a rabbit out of a hat—the wretched piece of cardboard on which I had written, "Don't forget to look under the mattress," with my name attached.

He thrust it under my nose and asked, "What's this mean?"

I gibbered at the thing, gave a feeble laugh and said it was a joke.

"What kind of a joke?" he asked, keeping his eyes on my face.

I had to tell him then. I said that the Bakers had lost a wallet and had searched the entire floor for it. I told him we had searched my room tonight and I had put the sign there for a joke.

He immediately wanted to see the Bakers, and I said I'd get them for him and backed out of the room before he could stop me.

Trevis was still in the solarium, and I told him in a hurry that the police were under the impression that the search of my room had gone on with my full knowledge and consent. He looked thoroughly uncomfortable, but he thanked me in a subdued voice—and had barely finished when he was captured and led away.

I poured out the dregs of the coffee and drank it—black and cold—and nearly choked to death when someone cleared a throat directly behind me.

It was Michael, and he kindly patted me on the back until I got my breath.

"I didn't know you were there," I said resentfully.

"Obviously."

"Why didn't you make a noise?"

"I thought you and Baker might go into a love scene."

I gave him a withering glance—and there was a short silence.

Michael broke it by saying in a voice of mild wonder, "What I can't make out is why you let those poor harried Bakers go on searching, when all the time you know where their wallet is."

CHAPTER EIGHT

"WHAT are you talking about?" I asked, staring at him. "I never saw their blasted wallet in my life."

"You searched your aunt's room, didn't you?" he asked with his eyes on my face.

"How did you know?"

"Miss Gould put it on the chart," he said, grinning faintly. "I believe she thought it indicated that the old lady was cracked."

"Isn't she?" I asked, yawning.

"Don't think you can get me to put it down in black and white, so that you can have her put away and get control of her money."

I said, "No—of course not. Because that would mean the loss of your fanciest customer."

"Exactly."

"What about the wallet?" I said impatiently. "Do you actually know where it is?"

"Do you mean to tell me that you searched that entire room—and didn't find it?"

"I searched every square inch," I said firmly, "and I'm willing to swear it wasn't in the room then. I'd have opened it up and looked through it if I *had* found it," I added reflectively.

"It's in the toe of one of your aunt's shoes," Michael said casually.

"But—"

"Did you look in the toes of your aunt's shoes?"

"No. I didn't suppose there'd be anything but cobwebs in the toes of her shoes."

He said, "It's a good thing your ambitions don't run to being a policeman. They'd keep you pounding a beat for the rest of your life."

"What business took you to the toe of Aunt Isabelle's shoe?" I asked resentfully.

He laughed quietly for a moment and then explained, "She sent me to the closet to get her hat. She wanted to see if it had been spotted with rain—and passed the remark that it didn't matter much, because she would never be well enough to wear it again anyway."

"What hat?" I asked suspiciously. "She taxied here in an ambulance with her hair in a pigtail."

He nodded. "But she had a moment of optimism before she left and told Edith Quinn to bring her hat—because miracles occasionally happen and who knew but she might walk out of the hospital on her own two feet. Edith wore it—as being the easiest way to transport it—and apparently got it rained on."

I laughed heartily at a mental picture of Edith in one of my aunt's hats. Aunt Isabelle has an air—and can get away with the most frightful-looking clothes. Her hats are always decorated with flowing plumesor else purple pansies and lavender satin ribbons.

"I went to the closet," Michael went on, "and in reaching for the hat I kicked over one of her shoes. A small black wallet fell out, and I noticed that it was initialed with a gilt B. I thought nothing of it at the time, of course; I simply replaced it and figured that your aunt's choice of a hiding place for her money was her own business."

I stood up and moved toward the door. "I'll go and get it," I said over my shoulder.

"Why don't you tell the Bakers?"

"I'll take it to them," I said carelessly.

"You mean you want to look through it and see what's in it first."

I ignored him and went out into the hall. The light was on in my room, and there were still some people there—and I caught a glimpse of poor Frances' quiet little figure, still stretched on the bed.

I went into the main hall and noticed that there was a strange nurse at the desk. I passed her without stopping and hurried on to my aunt's room—and discovered that Michael was right beside me.

I frowned at him, but he was not to be shaken off.

He said, "Your supposition is quite correct—I want to see what's in that wallet too."

We went in and found that Edith had returned to her post. Aunt Isabelle was awake, with two pillows behind her and an animated sparkle in her eye.

Ames Baker's nurse, Olive Parsons, was also present, and she and Edith were giving my aunt a voluble account of what had happened.

Olive dried up when she saw Michael and began to edge toward the door. Aunt Isabelle greeted us with bonhomie and promptly shut Edith up too. "Jessie and Michael can tell me the rest—you always spit when you get excited and try to talk. And give me a cigar."

"All right," said Edith. "I'm only the old family servitor. And those cigars will make you ill one of these days."

"I smoke them for my hay fever, as you very well know," Aunt Isabelle said in a fury. "And if you don't think I've been ill for the last ten years you've been taking my money under false pretenses."

"I'll tell the world," Edith muttered.

I stepped in hastily with a pacifying account of the night's events. I had to move my position a couple of times in order to block Michael, who was edging toward the closet.

I finished the recital, declared that I was dead tired and was going to bed and said good night. I turned abruptly, walked straight to the closet and opened the door. I pretended to trip, sprawled on the floor and pawed frantically at my aunt's shoes. I shook them and stuck my hand into the toes—but there was no wallet. And there were no other shoes in the closet. There were no slippers either—because Aunt Isabelle always kept them beside her bed in case of fire.

I heard her voice, raised in exasperation, "What in God's name are you doing there, girl?"

I got up and turned around to see three astonished faces—and Michael's, which wore a broad grin.

"Sorry," I said shortly, "I mistook the door. Thought it was the hall door—and I tripped over something."

This didn't go over—and I resented their skepticism. I remembered several occasions at my home when departing friends had walked into the hall closet with the mistaken idea that they were walking out of the front door. A beau of mine had once left me in a fury, via the hall closet, and he was so annoyed at having his exit ruined that he stayed there, sulking, for an hour.

However, Aunt Isabelle merely sent the two nurses out of the room and then asked me brusquely what I wanted in her closet. I protested innocence to high heaven—but she fixed me with a stony eye, and at last I broke down and told her everything, with Michael laughing on the sidelines until I nearly threw the box of cigars at his head.

Aunt Isabelle, wide awake now and highly entertained, was inclined to disbelieve me when I said that the wallet was no longer in her shoe. The wretched woman actually made me search the entire room again—and Michael was delegated to follow after me, because she declared that she no longer trusted me.

After I had finished I asked, dully, if I could go.

"No," she said, crushing out her cigar. "Now that I have you and Michael together I want to talk to you."

"Aunt Isabelle," I said pitifully, "it's after three o'clock and there's been a horrible accident—and I'm dead tired."

She said, "Be quiet. Michael, did you buy the ring?"

"Ring?" he repeated vaguely.

"Yes—certainly. The engagement ring."

"Oh—of course." He pulled a fancy-looking little box out of his pocket and opened it. "Beauty," he said, showing it to Aunt Isabelle. "And quite a bargain. I found I had enough left over to buy a stickpin." He pulled another sparkling object from his pocket and added, "I hope you don't mind."

I stretched my neck for a closer view and recognized the five-and-ten-cent quality of the gems—but Aunt Isabelle won't wear glasses although she needs them. She said, "They seem to be very fine—but you really should have brought me the change. I'll let it go this time—but I want you to remember in the future."

Michael said, "Yes, ma'am," and put the stickpin back into his pocket, and Aunt Isabelle handed the ring to me.

Edith Quinn walked in at that point with a muttered remark to the effect that she was not going to hang around in the hall any longer.

Aunt Isabelle gave her a look and said, "Stop mumbling, woman, and speak up. What did you say?"

Edith thought better of it and backed down. "I was just saying, it's queer that Frances should be found in Jessie's room. What possible business could she have there?"

"Perfectly legitimate business," Aunt Isabelle snapped. "I sent her there myself."

CHAPTER NINE

WE ALL STARED at her until she requested us, irritably, to stop gaping. "Edith had disappeared—probably off about her own business somewhere—"

"If ever I got away with that in your employ," Edith interrupted bitterly, "I'd be smart enough to get me a better job."

"Hold your tongue!" said Aunt Isabelle. "I was quite alone and I felt that someone should be with me, so I rang for the floor nurse. This Hoffman girl came along, but she said that she could not stay, so I sent her off to look for Jessie."

"Did she come back?" Michael asked. "Or did Jessie appear?"

"No. I could have been dying here and they would not have concerned themselves."

"What time was it when you sent her to my room?" I asked.

Aunt Isabelle thought it over and decided that it was sometime between eleven and twelve, but she could not say exactly.

Edith said, "Oh—then I was having my supper, of course. I suppose I'm still allowed to eat."

"Anyone who could keep you from your food would have to get up early in the morning," Aunt Isabelle said coldly. "If you had any sense you'd cut out one meal—you're spreading like a bush."

"Bush or no bush," said Edith shortly, "I'm not cutting out my meals."

I thought quickly and remembered that we had stopped playing bridge at about twelve-thirty. Frances had been sent to my room between eleven and twelve—and the Bakers had stopped their search at about eleven-thirty. I decided that Frances had probably gone to my room between half-past eleven and twelve.

"At what time do you go down for your supper?" I asked Edith.

"At eleven-thirty," she replied, flicking a glance of defiance at Aunt Isabelle—who raised her eyebrows and stared steadily at Edith's hips by way of return.

I said, "Aha!" rather absently.

"What do you mean by that?" Aunt Isabelle snapped.

Edith sniffed. "Her semiannual idea just pulled in probably."

"You're all wrong about Jessie," said my aunt—but her tone lacked its usual note of vigorous conviction. She added almost weakly, "Her school reports always gave her an average standing."

Edith explained it to her. "Pupils in private schools are never given below average reports when they have rich aunts."

I slipped out at that point and modestly left them to it.

Michael had departed a moment earlier and was waiting in the hall. I gave the ring back to him. "Jessie Warren," I said, "does not wear ten-cent rings."

"You're wrong about the price—it set me back a quarter." He placed the little box in the palm of my hand, closed my fingers over it and gave them a little pat. "You'll have to wear it occasionally—she'll want to see it on you."

"Which reminds me," I said, narrowing my eyes at him. "Why did you tell her you'd marry me?"

He laughed a little and took my arm, and we began to move slowly up the hall. "I don't know her well enough to refuse. And anyway, she told me you had already agreed—which aroused the chivalry in me."

"I couldn't refuse her," I said reasonably. "She has me down in her will."

"Easier for you than me. She practically told me it would mean the bread out of my mouth."

I laughed. "Dirty fortune hunter," I said. "What are you going to do when the wedding day dawns?"

"It's a whole year away," he explained. "But I have given it some thought—only it wasn't exactly the dawn that I was thinking about—"

I jerked my arm free and said hastily, "How did you wangle such a late date? Aunt Isabelle has always said of husbands that one in the hand was worth two in the bush."

"I said I wanted to wait until I could support you in the style to which she had accustomed you."

I laughed all the way up the hall.

When we got to my room we found a policeman and the new floor nurse. "We've moved your things into the next room," the nurse explained. "They want this one kept closed."

"Closed," I thought, "and they can't lock it—none of these doors have locks." I shivered a little as I followed her to the other room. She opened the door for me and I went in.

"Are you all right now?" Michael asked. "Because if you are I'll go."

I said, "You don't have to make a play for your bread and butter out of Aunt Isabelle's hearing."

"Right. I was forgetting." He went off after saying good-by, and the other two moved away after him. The nurse took time out to give me an odd look and to send one at Michael's retreating figure.

I closed my door, took one look at the empty, quiet room and went straight out into the hall again. The Baker doors were closed, and I turned restlessly toward the solarium, which was in darkness. I switched on the lights, but the place was still cheerless and somehow even menacing—and I went back to my room. I got into bed and made a determined effort to get to sleep, but it was quite useless. I felt overstimulated and jittery, and after about ten minutes I got up again and went out into the main hall.

The new nurse was at the desk and she greeted me practically with open arms. She admitted to being distinctly nervous. "You know," she said in a low voice and with a glance over her shoulder, "the police think it's murder."

"But—here—in the hospital. And who would want to murder poor Frances anyway?"

She said, "Oh, my dear! You don't know anything about the private lives of nurses. They may appear to be quiet and efficient and all that on the floor—but some of them are certainly hell-raisers on the outside."

"Have they any ideas about who did it?" I asked.

"No—I guess not. It seems she was hit over the head several times with something heavy and blunt."

"But couldn't it have been an accident?"

"If it was then somebody put her under the bed there after she was dead—and also cleaned up—or removed—the blunt instrument—and that doesn't make sense."

"No," I agreed thoughtfully.

"You know her boyfriend was in. He was all broken up—poor thing."

"What was he like?"

"Good-looking," she said and added, "Say—I see you're engaged to Doctor Rand."

"Where do you see it?" I asked.

"Well—I mean—I heard—"

"Where did you hear it?"

But she either could not or would not say, and at last I let it drop, without confirmation or denial, and presently wended my way back to my room.

It was about four o'clock, and the blackness was beginning to have a grayish cast. I left the door open, got into bed and discovered that I was drowsy and ready for sleep.

I was just dozing off when I distinctly heard the faint swish of the door from the main hall. My eyes flew open, and in the silence I heard quiet footsteps passing my door and retreating in the direction of the solarium. The sort of rubber or rubber sound that they gave made me feel sure that it was a nurse—but the state of my nerves demanded an investigation, and I switched on the light and got out of bed again.

The lights were out in the solarium, but the dawn was far enough advanced to enable me to see pretty clearly anyway. I had a moment of horror as I made out a nurse—slim and blonde and crouched down beside the chaise longue—but I shook it away almost immediately. Frances was dead—and a few moments of silent watching showed me that this one was making a very businesslike search of the solarium.

She stood up and moved toward one of the chairsand I caught a glimpse of her face. It was Olive Parsons.

CHAPTER TEN

I SAID, "Hello."

Olive jumped about three feet off the floor, spun around and stared at me.

"Jessie Warren," I said, "in person—or so they've always told me. And don't tell me—let me guess. You're looking for a small black wallet, initialed in gold with the letter B."

She put her hand over her heart and drew a couple of long breaths. "You nearly scared the pants off me. But how did you know?"

"About the wallet? It's the latest rave—everybody's looking for it—I am myself. So's old man Baker. Only he ought to wear something more than a nightshirt when he visits. Really, Olive—my aunt was embarrassed."

Olive had recovered her wind and her self-possession and she said firmly, "Your aunt had better be embarrassed for herself, rather than a poor old man who's very ill and doesn't always know what he's doing."

"Is he potty then?"

"No—but naturally he isn't quite normal—his illness, you see."

"Is he going to recover?"

A little frown appeared between her eyebrows, and she shrugged. "I don't know—maybe. But I wish we could set his mind at rest."

"What's he worrying about?"

"I don't know—but he's worrying plenty. The wallet, I suppose."

"Did he send you out here to look for the wallet?" I asked.

She nodded. "He keeps me searching for the damned thing constantly. In fact, half the time I'm wandering around when I should be looking after him."

I laughed. "Did you ever get within smelling distance of it?"

"No," she said disgustedly, "and I don't expect to. But he'll have kittens if someone doesn't find it for him pretty soon."

"I got close to it once," I told her. "Closer than you did."

Her dark eyes snapped and she said eagerly, "Where?"

"Michael said it was in the toe of my aunt's shoe—but by the time I got there it was gone."

She said, "Well, for heaven's sake!" and walked over to the chaise longue. I watched her burrow under the pillow, pull out a packet of cigarettes and light one for herself.

"Why don't you race along and look?" I asked.

She made a little face at me and shook her head and at the same time curled up in one of the chairs and puffed comfortably at her cigarette.

I thought she looked quite attractive. Edith had told me that she was nearly forty—and while I knew she was not particularly young I should have put her age at nearer thirty. Her hair was bleached, of course—but it was well done, and she had nice dark eyes and a creamy skin. Her mouth was large but it had character—and her figure was youthful.

She glanced at me and said, "No use my looking in your aunt's shoe if you say the thing isn't there any more."

I perched myself on the arm of a chair and swung my foot, with the slipper dangling on my toes. "It seems to be temperamental though," I suggested. "Perhaps it has returned to my aunt's shoe by this time."

She said, "Oh no—I don't think so," and blew smoke through her nostrils.

"Where were you during the excitement?" I asked presently.

"I got up here a couple of times—but I had to keep the whole thing quiet from Mr Baker. I had his door closed so that he wouldn't hear your aunt shouting about it."

"Apologies for my aunt," I murmured.

She widened her eyes and looked at me. "Well, after all, you can't help it—if she is an old pest."

"Let us," I said briefly, "leave my aunt out of it."

She crushed out her cigarette and stood up. "Better get back, I guess. The old man doesn't sleep any too well."

"Aren't you going to finish searching in here?"

"No—what's the use?"

"It's a logical place," I said thoughtfully. "At the other end of the building from my aunt's shoe."

"Do you mean that you think someone is hiding it on purpose?"

"It sounds a bit theatrical," I admitted, "but wallets can't play hide-and-seek without an escort."

"Well"—she shrugged and made for the door—"maybe it was stolen when the closet was cleaned," she suggested and disappeared into the hall.

It was quite light by that time, and my eyes were closing up, so I went back to bed and fell asleep at once.

I was awakened at eight o'clock by one of the maids, who informed me that my breakfast was waiting in the solarium. It was the first time she had shown me such consideration—as a rule she crept in quietly, put the tray down without a sound and sneaked off.

I dragged myself out of bed, put on a dressing gown and slippers and was halfway through my first cup of coffee before I fully woke up. I realized then that I had a lot more sleeping to do—and I hoped the coffee wouldn't keep me awake.

The Bakers appeared just as I was finishing, and I blushed for my appearance. They were all very neatly washed, brushed and dressed.

We exchanged greetings, and they sat down to their trays. Sheila messed around with hers for a while and then declared petulantly that everything was cold.

"It's your own fault," Gregg snapped. "The girl told you the breakfasts were here, but you had to go on fooling with your nails."

Sheila flung him a venomous look, and Trevis stepped in with a hasty change of subject. He began to talk about Frances and asked me several questions about what had happened.

Sheila was diverted from Gregg but she abandoned her food entirely, and once I saw her give a little shudder, as though she were afraid. She suddenly interrupted Trevis in midsentence, by putting her hands over her ears and saying shrilly, "If you say one more word about that ghastly affair I shall go into screaming hysterics."

Gregg ignored her and continued to munch toast, but Trevis patted her shoulder kindly and offered to talk about anything that pleased her.

She dropped her hands into her lap, closed her eyes for a moment and then opened them wide and looked at Gregg. He was still bumping a piece of toast around with his teeth.

In an effort to back up Trevis I introduced a new subject—and put my foot fairly and squarely into it. I merely asked, "Have you found your uncle's wallet yet?" and Sheila promptly went into the screaming hysterics with which she had threatened us.

I was a bit suspicious of the quality of her screams—but I did what I could to help. Gregg and Trevis got her to her bed, and I emptied a glass of cold water onto her face—which resulted only in bigger and better screams.

The floor nurse, Virginia Young, appeared suddenly in the room, and at sight of her Sheila stopped screaming almost immediately. I felt pretty sure at that point that the whole thing was an act.

Virginia seemed to think so too. She wore a cold and disapproving expression and she said, with the faintest hint of threat, "Well, well— we won't do this any more, will we?"

Sheila gave her a look, when she would have preferred, obviously, to slap her face, and snapped out a vicious demand for a cigarette. Trevis supplied her, and Virginia left the room—leaving an aroma of contempt.

I continued to stand by the window, until it dawned on me slowly that there was a sort of waiting silence. I glanced around hastily and saw at once that they were anxious to go into one of their conferences. I excused myself, and Trevis politely escorted me out.

I walked across the hall to my room and immediately tiptoed back and put my ear to their closed door.

Sheila was saying in a sulky tone, "Well—I thought if I got hysterical she might feel sorry for me and give us the wallet."

CHAPTER ELEVEN

I KEPT MY EAR to the door for a while, but I heard nothing more of interest so I went back to my room and got dressed. I wanted desperately to go to sleep again but decided that I'd better go down and look in on Aunt Isabelle to save a row.

She was asleep when I got there, so I murmured, "Thank God," and backed out again.

Miss Zimmerman followed me into the hall and seemed anxious to while the time away with a little chat. She had had all the details of the night's events from some of the nurses, but she insisted on having them again from me.

I delivered them—speaking rapidly and cutting corners—and then asked her about the cleaning arrangements of my aunt's room.

"Cleaning?" she said, blinking at me. "It's done by the hospital, you know. You don't have to bother about it."

"Yes, I know—but who does it? And when?"

"Has Miss Daniel complained?" she asked, looking worried. "It has always been quite satisfactory. Of course the room isn't done thoroughly while the patient is occupying—"

"Listen," I said hastily, "I merely want to know whether the room is cleaned once a day or twice a day—and who does it?"

"Oh," she said, "oh, I see. It's cleaned in the morning—that's all. Whatever made you think it was done twice?"

"Once, in the morning," I repeated thoughtfully. "Who does it?"

Miss Zimmerman began to get agitated. "I'm sure Miss Daniel has said something," she declared, wringing her hands. "Tell me, Miss Warren, *please.* I haven't seen any dust or dirt around myself—but Miss Daniel has such an eye for little things."

"I know all about her eye," I said impatiently, "but this has nothing to do with her. I want to know because I—well—I'm writing a book called *Hospitals as a Whole!*"

It was quite obvious by this time that she thought I was ready for the nearest asylum. She said faintly, *"Hospitals as a Hole?"*

"Miss Zimmerman," I pleaded. "All I want you to do is to lead me to the person or persons who clean my aunt's room."

She was very unwilling and still suspicious of my sanity, but in the end she led me through what seemed like several miles of hallways, alcoves and corridors, until we caught up with a huge, red-faced Irishwoman, wearing a blue-and-white-striped tent. A dark blue denim apron covered a very small portion of her facade.

Miss Zimmerman abandoned me at once and fled, murmuring something about getting back to my aunt, and I said good morning to the Irishwoman.

I got no response, so I came to the point at once and asked her if she had found a wallet in the toe of number twenty-five's shoe.

I thought she was going to hit me over the head with her mop, but she abused me verbally, instead, for several minutes. It seemed that she was an honest woman and that she had never in her life had the luck to run across any wallet—but if she ever did she would certainly turn it in on the spot. I thanked her and left in a hurry.

I promptly lost my way and I think I must have been over the entire building, trying to get back to familiar surroundings again. I spent quite a long time in the maternity wing and saw all the little babies in the nursery, crying their poor little heads off.

I solved it at last by going out into the street, via a side door, and walking around to the main entrance. From there I was able to get back to my aunt's room.

Miss Zimmerman was standing aimlessly in the hall.

"Patient still asleep?" I asked.

"Yes indeed. We're having a nice nap this morning."

"We wish we were," I said bitterly. I eyed her for a moment and tried to drop into a casual tone of voice. "Miss Zimmerman, did you find a wallet in the toe of my aunt's shoe?"

She gave me a peculiar look and said, "No."

"Are you sure?"

"I'm quite sure," she said firmly. "I know the Bakers are looking for a wallet, but I didn't know you were looking for one too."

"It's the same one," I explained, feeling a bit embarrassed. "I—I'm helping them."

"But why would it be in the toe of a shoe?"

Without any definite reason for it I felt that I did not want her to know about the wallet having been seen in the shoe. I said, "Well, I searched the room—but I didn't think of looking in my aunt's shoes."

"I don't believe a wallet would fit into the toe of a shoe," said Miss Zimmerman.

I took a long breath, counted ten and said patiently, "In this case, yes. The wallet is small and my aunt's shoes are average-sized rowboats."

We were interrupted by a roar from within, and Miss Zimmerman wasted her breath on a remark to the effect that Miss Daniel was now awake.

We went into the room, and Aunt Isabelle told us, in no uncertain terms, that she did not propose to be left alone all the time when she was paying out good money for nursing service. We suggested timidly that she had been sleeping—which threw her into a fresh temper. She said she hoped the time would come when Miss Zimmerman and I suffered from insomnia as she did—and when it did she further hoped there would be a couple of lying little wenches to tell us that we slept the clock around.

I was delivered by the arrival of a nurse, who told me that I was wanted at the desk. I went along to find one of the plainclothes men from the previous night awaiting me. His name was William Forrest, and he appeared to want a history of my life—as well as a complete repetition of last night's events.

I repeated the story of my discovery of Frances automatically—I had told it so often that I could have run it off in my sleep—but when we came to my life's history I wanted to know why.

Mr. Forrest explained impatiently that in a murder case they had to dig up everything they could.

I caught my breath sharply and repeated in a half whisper, "Murder!"

He curled his lip and asked, "What did you think it was?"

I considered that for a while and then admitted weakly, "Murder."

He was too disgusted to speak for a moment, so I asked, "Have you found the blunt instrument yet?"

"Who told you about it?"

"One of the nurses," I said hastily.

"No," he said. "We're looking for it."

I felt subdued and uneasy and I answered all his questions as best I could.

He said at last, "Your aunt wants you to marry Doctor Rand, doesn't she?"

I admitted it but added that we did not intend to carry out her wishes.

"Why not?" Nosy asked abruptly.

"We don't love each other," I said, feeling a bit of a fool.

"Is it true that Doctor Rand was interested in a blonde?"

"Is," I said, "not was. He had no interest in Frances, if that's what you mean."

"Who is she then?"

"I don't know."

"If you don't know," said William Forrest, "how can you say that it was not Miss Hoffman? She was a very beautiful girl."

"I know. But if Michael had been interested in Frances I should certainly have known about it. I've seen a great deal of both of them in the hospital—and there wasn't anything but indifference. I feel sure of it.

He kept his eyes on my face for a moment and then said unexpectedly, "Did you know that Frances Hoffman is the only blonde that Doctor Rand has taken out for the past six months?"

My mouth dropped and I stared at him. "No!" I breathed in amazement. "Do tell!"

He left me in what seemed to be a bit of a huff.

I thought it over for a while and came to the conclusion at last that he suspected me of being jealous of Frances and wanted to find out about it. I discovered, rather to my surprise, that my hands were clammy and my legs wobbly. I told myself, in a mild panic, that they *couldn't* think I'd murdered Frances.

It was nearly lunchtime, so I went along to the solarium and eased myself onto the chaise longue. Sheila was sitting in one of the armchairs, reading a book, and she raised her eyes for a moment to give me a brief "Hello."

I smoked a couple of cigarettes and thought about Michael and Frances. I could have sworn that they had been nothing to each other but doctor and nurse—Michael had never, at any time, appeared to give her a thought or a look. But, of course, you never could be sure about things like that.

Trevis, Gregg and the luncheon trays appeared together, and we all set to. After we had finished I suggested the coffee shop again, and they agreed.

We found Michael down there, fooling around with a sandwich and a cup of coffee. We sat down all around him and discoursed brightly on the modern books and plays—and for a while I forgot the sixth floor and all the mystery and trouble that were part and parcel with it.

Michael remained silent while we talked, his blue eyes remote and his mouth grim. Toward the end of our meal he glanced at me and announced brusquely that Aunt Isabelle was becoming almost too much of a nuisance to him.

"That's your worry," I said lightly. "You can't expect me to break into tears. At least you have your off hours."

He absently broke a match into four even pieces and said, "That's just the trouble. She's trying to control them too."

"I suppose," I said slowly, with my eyes on the broken match, "that you're upset about Frances."

He gave me a very blue stare for a moment of silence and then said, "What are you getting at?"

"Well, you—you went out with her, once or twice—"

"I have never," said Michael firmly, "been out with Frances Hoffman in my life."

CHAPTER TWELVE

WE HAD FINISHED our subsidiary luncheons, and the Bakers started to leave so I went along with them, but I hung back long enough to whisper to Michael that he had better have a word with me in private. He gave me a half-questioning, rather gloomy look but made no reply.

I went back to Aunt Isabelle's room fully prepared for a row because I had not given her more of my time—but she had something else on her mind.

As soon as I appeared in the doorway she said, "Have you heard, Jessie? Poor Mr. Baker! It seems he's dying."

I said, "Oh, I'm sorry. I understood that he was recovering."

"So did I. But these doctors make so many mistakes. Take my case, for instance—"

I did not want to take her case so I interrupted, "Are they sure he's dying?"

"Miss Zimmerman said Miss Cassidy told her there was really no hope for him."

I felt a sudden distaste for the subject and abruptly changed it to the first thing that came into my head. "How's Miss Zimmerman's love affair coming on?" I asked without really wanting to know.

My aunt reached for her smelling salts, took a long sniff and said, "It's off. I told her I'd discharge her if she had anything more to do with him—so she very sensibly sent him packing."

I glanced at Miss Zimmerman, who had just come in and was fooling swiftly around the room, as nurses will. I knew that she must have heard what Aunt Isabelle had just said, but she showed no consciousness of it—although her face was faintly flushed.

"What was wrong with him?" I asked loudly.

Aunt Isabelle made frantic signs to me to be quiet, but I pretended not to see them.

"What did you say was wrong with him?"

"Who?" asked Aunt Isabelle, still trying to save the situation.

"Miss Zimmerman's boyfriend," I said clearly.

Miss Zimmerman swung around and stared at me, the pink in her face deepening to a glowing red.

My aunt set the smelling salts down with a bang and said, "Take no notice of Jessie, my dear—she's talking at cross-purposes with herself—and since her birth she's been troubled a little with imbecility."

But I had made up my mind that Aunt Isabelle was not going to break up Miss Zimmerman's romance for no good reason. I looked straight at the girl and said, "I want to know why you broke with your boyfriend."

Miss Zimmerman pulled a clean, neatly folded handkerchief from her starched pocket, twisted it around in her hands for a moment and then, to my horror, used it to mop up a tear from each eye. She whispered, "Frances took him away from me," and ran out of the room, dropping more tears as she went.

Aunt Isabelle turned on me at once with a terrific word beating. She expressed a desire to slap me as well but said that she could not get out of bed and she supposed—and rightly—that I would not come over to her.

I let her rave while I sat and thought about Miss Zimmerman and bitterly regretted my blunder. I had supposed, of course, that Aunt

Isabelle, with her interfering ways, had simply broken up the romance for her own amusement—and I did not see why she should be allowed to get away with it. I wondered a little about Frances. Why should she take Miss Zimmerman's boyfriend when she had one of her own who, I knew, had absorbed her completely? And she was reported to have gone out with Michael too. It didn't make sense somehow.

I caught a glimpse of Michael through the half-open door, and he immediately made a sign to me to come out. I knew that he did not want to reveal himself, because it would mean something like an hour at Aunt Isabelle's bedside while she told him about her new and improved symptoms.

I stood up and drifted toward the door, but Aunt Isabelle pounced at once. "Where are you going now?" she yelled.

With the peace and quiet of the other patients on my mind I went back and began to smooth her pillow. I said, "There, there—don't excite yourself. I'm going to try and find Michael for you—I believe you're in a highly nervous state."

She gave me a shove that nearly sent me through the wall and shouted, "Hold your lying tongue! And leave my pillow alone. I'm getting sick and tired of your miserly duty calls—and I warn you that I have my will under the mattress, where I can get at it at any time." She narrowed her eyes and added, "You're not fooling me either. I know you're playing around with those Baker boys—and I think it's disgraceful when their uncle is dying."

I said firmly, "Aunt Isabelle, I must go to the bathroom and wash my hands. I shall be back within ten minutes."

She knew when she was beaten. She gave me a look and said, "The next time I come here I'll have a room with a bath."

I started toward the door and she called after me, "No matter how pretty those Baker boys are you're still going to marry Michael. Just bear that in mind."

Michael was pacing the hall restlessly. He pulled up in front of me and asked abruptly, "What is it you wanted to tell me? I'm going off now and I shall not be back here before tomorrow morning."

"Lucky hound," I muttered.

He made an impatient movement, and I said hastily, "It's just that the police think you went out with Frances on several occasions."

He looked at me. "That's what you wanted to tell me?"

I felt a bit abashed but I said, "Yes, that's all. I thought you'd like to know."

He fixed absent, somber blue eyes on my face for a moment and then, abruptly, he said, "Thanks," and walked off.

I thought him over for a while and then shrugged and decided that it did not much matter whether he had gone out with Frances or not.

My ten minutes were not yet up, so I went along to the desk and had a cigarette and a chat with Virginia Young.

"Vera Hackett will be on in Frances' place for a while," she told me. "There'll be fireworks for sure."

I laughed and thoroughly agreed with her. Edith and Vera Hackett had been bitter enemies since the days when they had trained together.

I asked Virginia if she had heard anything about Frances and Miss Zimmerman's steady, but she shook her head and declared that Frances had had her own boyfriend and was crazy about him. She was strongly of the opinion that Frances would not have gone out with another man.

"It's a terrible thing," Virginia said, frowning. "Who could have killed her? There was nobody here."

"Somebody might have come in from outside," I said thoughtfully. "It's easy enough. You can usually get by without being questioned if you look purposeful enough."

"Well—in the daytime, I suppose."

She had to go then, and I went back to Aunt Isabelle and was told that I had been a long time. Miss Zimmerman had gone off, and Miss Gould was sitting on a straight chair, knitting a yellow sweater.

I was kept at my aunt's bedside for the rest of the afternoon. I was very restless and very bored—and cigarettes were taboo. I got so desperate at last that I asked if I might have one of her cigars—this, after three sneezes on my part—two of them well done and the third badly executed.

Aunt Isabelle fell for it and told me to help myself—but the cigar was a flop. After two or three puffs I was so dizzy that Miss Gould and her sweater seemed to be swinging around me in slow wide circles.

I was finally released when Miss Gould returned from her supper at ten past six, and I flew along to the solarium, where the trays were already laid out.

There was no sign of the Bakers, and although I knocked on their doors they did not appear, so I ate alone. When I had finished with my tray I ate some of the things on the Baker trays.

I went into my bedroom then and started to read. When it got too dark after a while to see the page, I dropped the book and just lay there, because I was too tired to get up and put on the light.

I promptly went to sleep, and when I woke up again it was pitch dark and very quiet. As far as I could see through my open door the entire guest suite was in darkness. I had an instant vision of Frances' twisted little body stuffed crookedly under the bed in the next room—and the sweat sprang out on my forehead.

An impulse to spring up and turn on the light was frozen at its inception. In the stillness that beat so heavily on my ears I distinctly heard the squeaking of bedsprings in my former room.

CHAPTER THIRTEEN

I LAY QUITE STILL for a moment, while my heart raced madly. I knew the sound so well. When I had slept on the bed the spring had squeaked like that every time I moved. But who could be there? Surely not one of the nurses, when they all knew the room's gruesome story.

I strained my ears, but there was no further sound. I had a sudden horrid fear that the bed had squeaked when the unknown occupant had rolled out of it—and he might be approaching me now, in the dark, on tiptoes!

I scrambled to my feet and fled out into the hall and through the door into the main corridor. Vera Hackett was seated at the desk, and she gave me a cold stare of inquiry. She had always extended her feud with Edith through to me—but I had consistently ignored it and treated her as though we were friends.

"Get an orderly or someone," I gasped. "There's somebody in that room—where Frances was. Lying on the bed!"

She calmly unscrewed a fountain pen, capped the end and began to write. "I'm sure there's no need to get excited, Miss Warren," she said with her eyes on the paper. "It's probably one of the nurses taking forty winks. You would not know about it—but nursing is quite an arduous occupation."

"Are the nurses permitted to wink in the guest suite?" I asked, losing my temper.

Vera brought her fountain pen to a stop and lost a small fraction of her chilly aplomb. "Well—of course—"

"If it's a nurse she has no right to be there," I said, "and I want her put out."

Vera was short and plump, but her lips were thin. She folded them in and gave me a look that said very plainly, "The selfish meanness of the idle rich!"

She knew as well as I did that it would not have concerned me if every nurse on the floor spent the entire night in the guest suite, snoring loudly. But I was determined to have the place searched and I was too scared to do it alone.

There was a moment of silence, while we stared at each other with cold fury—and then Edith appeared quietly on her rubber-soled feet. She ignored Vera and said to me, "You're wanted."

"Edith," I said desperately, "will you come with me and search the guest suite? There's someone who has no business there—and Vera won't help me."

"Sure," said Edith matter-of-factly. She flicked a glance at Vera and added, "I'm not afraid."

We turned away from the desk together, and Vera called after us, "Why should you be? Any kidnaper would drop you at the first lamp-post—presupposing he had a large enough truck to transport you that far."

"Where does she think she gets off?" Edith muttered in a vexed undertone. "She's getting big as a house herself."

We went through the door into the guest suite, and I felt as though my stomach were dropping away from me. I clawed for the electric switch and was in a sweat of fear before I found it and turned it on. The hall was empty, and the door to my former bedroom was closed. I explained to Edith, in a whisper, about the bedsprings, and she said, "All right—we'll look in there first."

The room was empty. We looked in the bathroom, the closet and under the beds—but there was nothing.

"You're right though," Edith said slowly. "Somebody has been lying on that bed."

The beds had been freshly made up—but the one I had used was crumpled and the pillow flattened.

I shivered, and Edith said, "Come on—no use standing around. But somebody certainly has a nerve."

We made a hasty search of the solarium and my bedroom but found nobody. I stared at Edith, with my breath coming fast, and said, "It must be here still. I was outside the door all the time and no one came through."

Edith shrugged. "Where are the Bakers?"

"I don't know," I said, pushing my hair away from my hot face and looking uneasily around the room. "Aren't they down with the old man? I heard he was dying."

"They were not there when I passed," she said. "Olive was alone with him."

We listened and then tapped at the two Baker doors, but there was no answer and no sound. We pushed the doors open and peered in, and as far as we could see—the two rooms were empty. Edith refused to go in and search them, because she said it would be too awkward if she were caught. I tried to persuade her, but she would not consent and I had to let it go. I was too scared to do it by myself.

"As a matter of fact, though," Edith said, "you can get in and out of the guest suite without going through the door. I'll show you."

She took me back to the solarium and showed me a window which opened onto a fire escape. "Stick your head out," she said, "and you can see another window at the other end of the platform. It opens into the hall. We used to use it sometimes when we were in training and wanted to snatch a little extra sleep. Anyway, don't get yourself all in a dither over it. Push the bureau in front of the door when you go to bed and you'll be safe enough."

"Maybe," I said bleakly. "But, better still, perhaps I can persuade Aunt Isabelle to go home."

"You won't do that just now," Edith declared. "She's never had such an interesting visit—and nothing could drag her away in the middle of it."

"There's something horrible about that," I said, wrinkling my nose.

Edith raised her shoulders and her eyebrows and let them drop again. "Why? Suppose you were an old woman for whom no one has ever cared very much. You'd have to be interested in something, wouldn't you?"

"Well—but if she had less interest in the misfortunes of other people perhaps she'd be better liked."

"Don't get philosophical," said Edith. "It doesn't become you and you haven't the brain for it. As for your aunt, she has the money to buy interest for herself—and she isn't all mean either. She's busy right now, pushing you into an advantageous marriage."

"What do you mean," I said, outraged. "If Michael Rand is an advantageous marriage—I want to know about it."

"Save your breath," she said placidly. "You know very well you'd like to hook him—but he's never shown any interest in you."

"That's because I have red hair," I said bitterly.

"Well, cheer up—you'll get him. And if you could manage always to wear a hat in front of him he wouldn't notice the hair."

We started back toward Aunt Isabelle's room, and I began to think about Michael. I realized for the first time—and with a queer little feeling of discomfort—that I wanted him. I wondered whether it was my aunt's strong will working on me—or natural inclination. In any case, I decided to phone Lenore and tell her to bring over a couple of hats.

Ames Baker's room was quiet, and we saw Olive Parsons reading under a shaded lamp. She put the book down when she saw us and came to the door. "What's new?" she asked.

She was evidently all set for a little chat, but I could see that Edith wanted to get away, and I wanted to hurry through my duty call on Aunt Isabelle and go to bed myself.

Olive was not to be put off, however. She chattered along, and every time we tried to terminate the conversation she started it again.

I gave it up at last and asked her if she knew where all the Bakers were hiding.

"Why, you know, that's funny," she said. "The old man is worse tonight."

"I heard that he was dying," I said tentatively.

"Oh no—not quite that." She gave a little shiver. "He is worse though."

"Do the Bakers know?" I asked.

She nodded. "They were told this afternoon—and it seems they left almost right away."

"Left!" I repeated, stunned.

"Oh, not for good. They're coming back, but I don't know when."

"At what time did they leave?"

"Miss Gould saw them go off at about four o'clock—and as far as I know they haven't come back yet."

The old man stirred and moaned a little just then, and Olive turned away and went quietly to his bed.

Edith and I made good our escape and walked on to the corner room. We slowed down at the door and went in on tiptoes, taking care to make no noise in case Aunt Isabelle were sleeping.

But we need not have bothered, because she wasn't there.

CHAPTER FOURTEEN

WE JUST STOOD THERE for a while, looking at the empty bed—and then Edith flew to the closet and jerked the door open, while I looked feverishly behind the screen and under the bed.

But Aunt Isabelle very definitely was not in the room, and Edith and I, meeting at the washbasin, stared at each other in consternation.

"Maybe she went downstairs to complain at the office about being left alone so much," Edith said weakly and without conviction. "Only where would it get her? She'd never fire me."

"Why not?" I asked curiously.

"Because I can take her entire collection of insults without bursting into tears. Besides, I think I'm the only employee she's ever had who was willing to stay longer than a month. I even took her hot-water bottle once when I had a toothache, and it seems she had cold feet and was looking for it all night. She nearly broke my eardrums over it—but she didn't fire me."

I said, "All right—so she won't fire you. But she must be found, and we can't waste time standing here talking about it. Come on."

We went out into the hall and straight along to the desk where Vera still sat, pushing her fountain pen around. I asked her if she'd seen my aunt Isabelle passing recently.

She gave me a look in which she managed to express her opinion of young girls indulging in strong drink and declared that Miss Daniel was in her room, where she belonged.

"Would you care to bet on that?" Edith asked.

But it seemed that Vera had the same contempt for gambling that she had shown for my supposed inebriation. "Taking a poor old lady for your subject!" she added virtuously.

"Then you haven't seen her?" I said impatiently.

"How could I? She is confined to her bed, and she's *supposed* to have her own private nurse in attendance."

I controlled my temper and asked, "Which rooms are vacant in the corridor?"

Vera, willfully misunderstanding me, sent her gaze along the corridor that ran past the elevators and contained the more moderate-priced private rooms. "They are all occupied, except—"

"Can't you forget your spite for about five minutes?" I asked wearily. "Of course I mean this hall—"

"If you'll just turn your head to the left," Edith said with false courtesy, "you'll see it. Quite a broad corridor—with doors opening off into the deluxe rooms. Somebody should have told you about it."

"Listen, Vera," I said seriously, "you'll probably get into trouble yourself if we don't find her."

She flicked me a venomous glance, but I thought she was a bit uneasy. After a moment's silence she said briefly, "Miss Daniel in sixty-five and Mr. Baker in sixty-three. The rest are unoccupied."

Edith and I hurried off and searched the empty rooms—turnabout, and with one of us always waiting out in the hall—but without result. We went back and searched my aunt's room again, but she was still missing, and I began to be thoroughly alarmed.

We went to Mr. Baker's room and signaled to Olive, who came quietly to the door. Edith explained the situation in a rapid whisper, and Olive exclaimed softly, "My God! Edie—you're in for some trouble!"

"I've had trouble before," Edith said shortly. "Go and look in the closet, Olive—and under the bed. Just make sure she isn't there."

Olive said, "I know she isn't, but I'll look anyway."

We watched her make a silent, hasty search, and then she came back to the door, shaking her head. "She's not here, girls. I think you ought to notify the office."

Edith shrugged and turned away. "I guess we'll have to," she said reluctantly.

"Can't we look anywhere else?" I asked anxiously and was conscious that my heart was pounding.

"Loads of places—but it takes too much time. I'm afraid—"

"Let's look through the guest suite again," I said suddenly. "She might have gone along there to give me hell about something."

Edith nodded. "O.K. But if she isn't there I'll have to turn in the alarm."

As we passed at the desk Vera raised her head and called after us in a distinctly worried voice, "Where is she? Have you found her?"

"Sure," said Edith. "She was getting a manicure."

The guest suite was in complete darkness, and as I groped for the hall switch I said uneasily, "I thought we left the hall light on."

I pressed the switch, and the hall remained in darkness.

"Damn!" Edith muttered beside me. "We did leave it on—I guess the bulb is broken."

We edged our way in the darkness to my room, and I felt a little thrill of relief as a flood of light responded to my clammy fingers on the switch.

"Nobody here," Edith said, glancing about. "We'd better look in that next room."

I nodded mutely, and she said, "I'll do it. You wait in the hall—and if she shows up, for God's sake, hogtie her and yell for me."

I laughed—a thin, hysterical sound that ended in a shudder—while Edith walked determinedly to the door of the next room and pushed her way in.

I stood in the hall, in the light that came from my room, and felt as though my legs were made of spaghetti.

Edith came out presently—her face gray and drops of moisture on her forehead. "Not there," she said and added, "God! That room gives me the creeps."

She closed the door firmly. "Your turn now. You do the solarium, and I'll stay in the hall."

I walked into the solarium, sweating, but anxious to get it over, and turned on several lights. I could see, almost at a glance, that the place was empty, but I made a sketchy search—my shoes making a hollow clatter on the stone floor. I was beginning to wish that we had gone straight to the office and reported Aunt Isabelle as missing. At any rate, I wanted to get out of the guest suite. The place horrified me, and I did not feel that I could ever sleep there again.

Edith poked her head in at the door and said, "Come on—she isn't there. We'll do the Baker rooms."

I joined her in the hall, and she promptly disappeared into the bedroom occupied by the Gregg Bakers. She was out again almost immediately, shaking her head. "Nothing doing in there."

She indicated Trevis' room. "Go on. It's our last chance."

I pushed at the door and eased myself into the room. The door swung to behind me and closed with a gentle swish. I stood for a moment in impenetrable blackness and then raised a shaking hand and began to grope along the wall for the electric switch. My fingers had just touched the cool metal of the plate when, in the heavy darkness, I distinctly heard someone draw a labored, snoring breath.

My finger pressed the switch automatically, and the room sprang into light. I huddled against the wall, the back of my hand pressed against my mouth, and stared, blinking, at the beds.

Sheila Baker lay on one of them. Her eyes were not quite closed, and she appeared to be looking at me through the slits. She said nothing and made no movement.

I gasped and precipitated myself into the hall, where I grabbed feverishly at Edith's arm. "Sheila Baker!" I jabbered. "You'd better come and see. She—she looks queer."

Edith followed me, and we pushed into the room again. As we approached the bed Sheila said something in a thick mutter that was quite unintelligible. Edith bent over her while I hung on the back of a chair, and after a moment she straightened abruptly and said, "Boiled!"

"But—"

"High as a kite."

Sheila spoke again, more clearly: "This isn't Gregg's bed, ish it?"

Edith said, "No, it isn't. Have you seen Miss Daniel?"

Sheila laughed for quite a while and then stopped suddenly, and an anxious expression appeared on her face. "It's not Gregg's room? You shaid it wasn't. I'll never sleep in Gregg's room again." She raised her head from the pillow and said belligerently, "I'm going out."

Edith pushed her back. "Why don't you want to sleep in Gregg's room? It's a nice room."

"Oh yes—I know. Nice room. It's a nice room. It can be as nice as hell! I won't—"

Edith glanced at me and then made a deliberate attempt to snoop. "I don't blame you," she said to Sheila. "Wasn't he awful?"

"Filthy!" Sheila muttered. "And after that he expects me to sit in there and wait until he comesh back."

"He shouldn't have gone," Edith suggested hopefully.

Sheila rolled her head from side to side. "He shouldn't have gone. Of course he shouldn't have gone. One of them should have stayed with me—let the other go. I can't stand it—stay here all alone. Only a little while ago somebody crept up behind her—killed her—hit over the head. And I'm supposed to stay here till they do the same to me."

She began to cry, and Edith looked at me and said, "Get me a glass of water. Maybe we can get her to talking."

"What about our honor?"

"You take care of your honor," said Edith, "and I'll look after mine. Go and get the water."

I opened the door to the bathroom and stepped in. It was brilliantly lighted, and Aunt Isabelle, erect in dressing gown and slippers, stood in front of the washbasin, glaring at me.

CHAPTER FIFTEEN

FOR A MOMENT of blank astonishment I simply gaped at her, and then I said stupidly, "What on earth are you doing here?"

Her eyes blazed with fury, and I thought she was going to slap me. I edged away a step and became more tactful. "Edith and I have been absolutely frantic—looking everywhere and knowing all the time that you are barely able to stand."

I could see her temper ease off a bit, but her eyes were dark with suspicion. "Where were you?" she demanded in a fierce whisper. "Do you think I can lie in that bed hour after hour with no one attending me?" Inspiration moved me, and I lied swiftly, "We were having a conference about your case with Michael and another doctor. You'd better come back to bed now."

"I can't go through there," she whispered crossly. "That woman trapped me in here—and I don't want her to see me."

"Why not? You can say you were looking for me."

"I don't tell lies," she snapped, "and I wasn't looking for you."

"Then what *were* you doing?" I asked simply.

To my surprise she actually lost her poise for a moment and looked a bit confused. But she rallied quickly. "I was looking for a four-leafed clover," she said bitterly. "Stop your silly chatter and get me back to my bed, before I collapse."

"Well, come on then," I said, taking her arm. "You need not worry about Mrs. Baker—she's dead drunk."

"Drunk?" my aunt whispered with alert interest.

"Yes."

The door opened suddenly, and Edith stood staring at us.

Aunt Isabelle frowned at her. "Close your mouth, woman. I've no interest in your dental work."

Edith closed her mouth and then opened it again to say briskly, "Well, suppose we get back to bed."

"Suppose I do what I please and you go to the hot place," Aunt Isabelle retorted.

"I've been there ever since I entered your employ," Edith replied, undisturbed. "Do you want me to help you back to your bed? Or will you make it under your own steam?"

Aunt Isabelle backed down, as she often did when Edith showed fight. "Kindly assist me," she said coldly. We walked her out of the bathroom and through the bedroom. Sheila watched us in silence until we reached the door, when she suddenly cried shrilly, "No! You can't leave me—I won't stay here alone—with that other thing!"

"What does she mean?" I whispered. "What thing?"

"For God's sake, stay with her, Jessie," Edith said, "while I get this one to bed. I'll send Vera in to fix her up."

I fell back reluctantly. "Send Vera in right away then. I don't know what to do for her, and I don't like being alone with her."

"I'll send her right along," Edith promised, and Aunt Isabelle butted in with, "You'll first attend to me."

They went off, and I glanced warily at Sheila and then began restlessly to pace the room. I swore to myself that I would not spend the night in that guest suite—if it meant that I had to ask Aunt Isabelle to move over!

It was half-past one, and the night was hot and close and breathless. I continued to pace the room, until I noticed that Sheila's eyes followed me wherever I went with eerie persistence. I couldn't stand it after a while, so I sat down on her bed and tried to talk to her.

"Are you feeling better?" I asked.

Her eyes left my face and slipped around the room.

"I know—I'm drunk. I'm very drunk." Her eyes closed, and I thought she had dropped off to sleep, but she presently opened them again with a childish whimper. "I have to get drunk—can't help it—they go off and leave me here alone—with that thing."

I took a hasty glance about the room, swallowed a couple of times and asked shakily, "What do you mean? What thing?"

She moaned and beat softly on the bed with her clenched fist. "It's in here—somewhere. It's been here all night."

"That's ridiculous," I said too loudly. "We've just finished searching the entire guest suite—and there's no one here but you and me."

Sheila rolled her head from side to side, and two small sparkling tears welled at the corners of her eyes and dropped onto the pillow. "It might have gone away for a while—it does that sometimes. But it will come back."

"You probably heard something," I said uneasily. "But it was only my aunt Isabelle. She was in here for some time."

"Oh no," said Sheila, "her—she was just looking for it, like the rest of them."

"When did she come in?"

"A little while ago. I was glad, because then I wasn't alone any more."

"I don't see why you stayed here if you were so frightened," I said after a moment. "You could have gone out into the main hall. Vera Hackett is a bore, but at least she would have been company."

"No, no—they wouldn't let me—they told me—must stay here. Someone might come in and look for it . . . ." Her voice trailed off, and she closed her eyes again.

I thought it over for a while and then asked, "Did Aunt Isabelle find it?"

She did not answer and she appeared to me to be sleeping. I got up and went to the door and looked out into the dark hall—but there was no sign of Vera. I left the door open, in the hope of a stray breeze, and began to pace the room again—mentally cursing both Edith and Vera.

Two or three minutes must have passed in a dead silence that was broken only by my own quick, restless footsteps—and then I noticed that Sheila's eyes were following me again. I shivered and resumed my seat on the bed. It seemed to me that in her condition she should long ago have gone off into a drunken sleep that would last until morning.

I looked at her and asked almost fretfully, "Why don't you go to sleep?"

"I mustn't."

I wandered to the door again but there was still no sign of Vera, and I presently returned to the bed, because I could not stand Sheila's eyes following me.

She said, "I never saw so much red hair in all my life—two or three of you—with red, red hair—it fills the room. It's so bright it hurts my eyes."

"Oh, be quiet," I said crossly. "It's not as bad as that."

"Oh yes—it is. Worse. Room's on fire." She began to laugh.

"Stop it!" I said sharply and watched her anxiously. I did not want her going hysterical on me.

The laugh came to a jerky stop, and I asked hastily, "When are they coming back?" I had given up all hope of Vera.

"Not until tomorrow. They both had to go because they don't trust each other, you see."

She giggled, and I said, "Where did they go?"

"The house, of course."

"And they're going to spend the night there?"

"It's such a big house—it takes time to search a big house—it takes all night." She gave me a wide-eyed stare and added very earnestly, "Trevis is much nicer than Gregg."

Well, I thought so, too, but I asked curiously, "Why?"

She turned her head away and seemed not to have heard, and I wondered why Gregg and Trevis were searching a big house and whether Sheila still preferred Trevis when she was sober. Further, what connection did Sheila's preference for Trevis have with the fact that Trevis and Gregg were searching a big house—if any? I supposed that they were still after the black wallet—and mentally cursed Michael for a fool for not having investigated its contents when he had the thing in his hand.

I glanced at Sheila and felt the hair stir all over my head. She was staring fixedly over my shoulder at the open door behind me, and her eyes were dilated with horror.

CHAPTER SIXTEEN

I SPRANG TO MY FEET and whirled around—and saw nothing but the open door and the black hall beyond. I walked to the door on shaking legs and forced myself to look out—but I could see nothing, and everything was perfectly quiet.

Sheila began to whimper. "I can't stand it—I'm going crazy. I don't care what they say—I've got to get out of here."

I went back to her. "What did you see, Sheila?" I asked. Her body was shaking and her teeth chattering. "It follows me around," she whispered. "I can't get away from it—it's always there, somewhere. And it comes and looks at me."

I huddled against the footboard and asked in a voice that I tried to keep normal, "What is it? A man?"

"Oh no—not a man. Not— It's a thing."

"Don't be silly," I said loudly, trying to reassure myself as well. "What do you mean by a thing? What is a thing?"

"I don't know," she moaned, moving her head restlessly on the pillow. "I don't know—I don't know."

"What does it look like?" I persisted.

"I don't know—nothing—nobody. It has no face—just an old slouchy, squashy body—and no head."

I felt the perspiration spring out on my forehead but I said firmly, "That's just silly—and you ought to pull yourself together."

She gave a bitter little laugh. "That's what Gregg says. Easy for him—he hasn't seen it."

I was vastly relieved, at that point, to hear competent rubber-soled footsteps approaching from the hall, and Vera presently appeared in the doorway.

"As if I didn't have enough to do, looking after the patients, without this. Really!" She looked at Sheila. "Disgraceful! A young, refined-looking woman like that!"

"Too much of this modern freedom," I said, shaking my head. "Also, and specifically, too much scotch."

Vera curled her lip and said, "Give me a hand here."

I helped her to get Sheila undressed, and then, of course, we had no nightgown for her.

"In the next room," I said to Vera—determined not to go after it myself.

"Isn't this her room?"

"No—but I can't see moving her in that state. I'll stay with her while you go and get the nightgown."

Vera went off, grumbling. But she had not heard about Sheila's Thing—and so could not be afraid of it. She didn't meet up with it, apparently, for she presently returned with a nightgown, and I helped her to get Sheila into it.

I fled then. I did not intend to be left with Sheila again, and I figured that Vera would have to get away from her as best she could.

I went swiftly through the darkened hall and out of the guest suite— and drew a long quivering breath of relief.

I headed for Aunt Isabelle's room, because I had nowhere else to go—and I had made up my mind to do my sleeping by daylight. I glanced in at Mr. Baker's room, and saw Olive sitting by the shaded lamp with some knitting. The work had dropped into her lap, however, and she was staring across the bed. I knew how bored she must be and decided never to be a nurse.

Aunt Isabelle was snoring loudly, and Edith lay in the armchair, with her feet up, sleeping more quietly.

I hesitated for a moment and then turned away. There was no sense in sitting on a straight chair and listening to them sleep.

I looked in at Olive again, in the hope that she might want to keep me company—but she was still staring into space, so I left her to it. I noticed that the iron handle which was used to crank the bed into a sitting position was lying on the floor. I murmured, "Shiftless," and passed on.

Vera was back at her desk, and I wandered up and asked, "How on earth did you get away?"

"Mrs. Baker is sleeping," she said briefly.

"Sleeping?" I repeated in surprise. "She wouldn't go to sleep for me. She told me she mustn't."

"You have no professional training, Miss Warren."

I admitted it and dropped wearily into a chair. I knew Vera didn't want me there—her attitude said so very plainly—but I could not face the guest suite. It was twenty minutes past two, and I wondered how I could possibly spend the rest of the night sitting around doing nothing or forcing Vera to talk to me.

She was scratching away busily with her fountain pen, and I said idly, "You ought to have more help on this floor at night."

She put the pen down, opened the floodgates and deluged me with her grievances. Dirty politics, malice, jealousy, sheer bad luck, had all had a poke at her from time to time. Through it all her head remained bloody but unbowed, and a woman might be down but she was never out.

It was more boring than doing nothing. I put up with it until one of the room lights went on and she had to go, and then I decided that I could stand it no longer and that I'd have to go into the guest suite and sleep along with Sheila and the Thing.

I went at once—before I had time to think too much about it—and groped my way through the dark hall to my bedroom. I turned on the light, made a hasty search and then rolled the bureau in front of the door. I undressed, turned out the light and got into bed.

I had hoped that I would go straight to sleep—and found, instead, that I was wide awake. I smoked a cigarette and tried again—but it was no use. I was terribly tired, too—so tired that I could not keep my eyes open—and yet when I closed them and lay there quietly my brain became acutely active.

I found myself thinking of Frances and how she had been stuffed under the bed—and then I had to get up and turn on the light and look under the beds again.

There was nothing, of course, and I told myself not to be a fool.

And then, quite clearly, I heard the squeak of bedsprings in the next room.

CHAPTER SEVENTEEN

FOR A MOMENT I had to battle a rising feeling of sheer panic—and then I began to pace up and down. *Somebody* was in that damned room—

and how could it be Sheila when Vera had left her sleeping? And if it was not Sheila then who *could* be there? Unless it was Sheila's squashy, headless Thing.

I tried to tell myself not to be a fool, but the idea started the feeling of panic whirring up inside me again. I could not stand my room for another instant, and I pushed the bureau away from the door and went straight across to Trevis' room. Sheila was still there, and she appeared to be in a deep sleep.

I turned away, fled through the dark hall and out the door into the main corridor. I had a faint sense of guilt at having left Sheila alone in that horrible guest suite—but it was pretty faint.

Vera was at the desk, and she greeted me with raised eyebrows. "If I had your luck I'd be sleeping and enjoying it," she said acidly.

"Not in that guest suite—you wouldn't," I muttered.

"Have you a complaint?" she asked coldly.

"Only that there's someone in that room again. The one where Frances was murdered."

"Murdered!" she repeated with a little shriek.

"Surely you knew?"

"Certainly not!" she gasped. "I thought there'd been an accident."

"No," I said shortly, "no accident. Now how about getting someone to find out who's lying on that bed?"

She tapped with her fingernails on the edge of the desk and said, "Well—I don't know how you could possibly hear the sound of bed-springs in the next room—particularly when your door was closed with a bureau against it."

"And I'm telling you that I heard it," I said firmly. "I couldn't mistake that sound if I heard it in Grand Central Station. I slept on the bed and I know that it lets out a falsetto squeak when you move around on it. Somebody—or some moving object is on that bed!"

Vera drew a sharp, vexed sigh and stood up. "I shall ask to be transferred," she said and began to move toward the guest suite.

I went, too, because my conscience insisted on it—and anyway, I don't believe she would have gone if she had not heard me behind her. "Ask for the psychopathic ward," I suggested. "It'll be a nice rest for you."

She clattered briskly through the door but came to a dead stop when she found that the hall was dark. "Where's the light here?" she demanded.

"Broken. But don't worry—the hospital will probably get around to it by next fall."

Her assurance faltered, and she asked, "Well—but where can we get some light?"

"Wait a minute," I said. "I'll open my door—the light's on in there."

I stuck my head into my room and looked around fearfully—but it appeared to be quite peaceful and exactly as I had left it. I set the door wide, and the light streamed out into the hall.

Vera took a long breath, straightened her cap and plunged into the next room—and I followed close behind her.

It was pitch dark, but we managed to find the switch after a bit of groping and turned on the light.

The room was neat, orderly and empty—and the beds were smoothly made up, without so much as a wrinkle on their starched counterpanes.

Vera sniffed and walked to the bathroom, while I looked under the beds and in the closet. Nobody, of course. But on the floor under one of the beds I found a small, obviously inexpensive bottle of perfume, with the seal unbroken. I turned it over in my hand curiously. It was not mine, and I wondered how it could have got there. Certainly not from the pockets of poor Frances' uniform—for I knew that the police had gone through the room with a fine-tooth comb—and such a thing would never have been overlooked.

I held the little bottle up and said to Vera, "Is this yours?"

She glanced at it briefly. "Certainly not. At my age! I leave that sort of thing to old fools like Edith Quinn."

I dropped it into my pocket and followed her out of the room; I saw that she was making for the hall door, and I asked hastily, "Aren't we going to look through the rest of the rooms?"

"Miss Warren, I have work to do and I simply cannot spend the rest of the night holding your hand."

I said, "God forbid. But won't you at least take a look at Mrs. Baker before you go?"

She altered her course and went to Trevis' room, where we found Sheila still sleeping peacefully.

"I'll leave the light on," Vera said, "so that she won't be scared if she wakes up."

"Is she likely to wake up?"

"No, no. She'll sleep till morning."

"Then why in hell," I asked blankly, "do you want to waste the electricity?"

She ignored me and swished her way out to the main hall and back to the desk—and I followed close at her heels.

I offered her a cigarette, and she refused as a matter of course. But by this time I think she had come to the conclusion that I was just another of the dirty lefts dealt her by fate, and apparently she made up her mind to accept me. She told me a long tale about a man who was, and always had been, in love with her—but he had a wife and twins— which meant that there wasn't much hope for Vera. After a brief pause for station identification, she started in on another story—this one about her niece, who was on the verge of marrying the wrong man.

I stopped her and told her I'd heard it, and while her mouth was still hanging open I murmured that I wanted to look in on my aunt— and made my escape.

Aunt Isabelle's snores were audible some distance up the hall, and when I got to her room I saw that Edith was still sleeping soundly in her chair—this time with her mouth wide open. I felt an impulse to go in and close it—but controlled myself and turned away.

I started slowly back and looked in at Mr. Baker's room, wondering if Olive were ready for a little conversation. But she was still staring into space, with her knitting lying in her lap, and I wondered if she were doing some sort of nurse's trick of napping with her eyes open so that she could not be accused of sleeping on the job.

I tested her by clearing my throat, but she made no move. I noticed, however, that she had picked up the handle and put it back into its groove at the foot of the bed.

I moved on slowly. Vera was not at the desk, and the white framed clock that was set into the wall above it showed the time to be ten minutes to four. I sighed and reflected that a night could seem like a week when you were trying to do away with it.

I squared my shoulders and went through the door into the guest suite. Light streamed from Trevis' room and from mine, and I felt my overstimulated nerves quiet down a little. I even walked down to the solarium and turned on the lights there. It looked vast and empty—but it was refreshingly cool. Most of the windows were open, and there was an occasional breeze. I sat down in one of the wicker armchairs and had a cigarette—and felt very brave indeed.

The silence was profound, and after a while I began to feel that perhaps I was being unnecessarily foolish. "After all," I thought, "it would be better to smoke my cigarette in my own room, with the bureau against the door—where I'm safe from the intruders—including squashy Things."

I got up quickly and, with growing panic, raced along to my room and closed the door with a bang. I pushed the bureau in front of it and then—rather belatedly, since I was barricaded in—looked in the bathroom and closet and under the beds.

I drew a little breath of relief that was sharply cut off. One of the handles that was used to wind the bed up and down was out of its groove and lying on the floor.

CHAPTER EIGHTEEN

I STARED at the handle for a while, trying to remember what was familiar about it—and then it came to me. I had seen one lying on the floor in Mr. Baker's room too—only it had subsequently been returned to its proper place.

I picked the thing up and looked at it and then stooped and fitted it into the socket where it belonged. I jiggled it around a bit, but it seemed to be firm enough, and I felt pretty sure that it could not have fallen out by itself. Which meant that someone must have taken it out and dropped it on the floor—and there wasn't any sense to be made out of that.

I left the light burning, climbed wearily into bed and tried to put the whole thing out of my mind—although I could not help wondering, fretfully, why they did not put ordinary beds in the guest suite.

It was still very hot, and I tossed restlessly for a while, but I was getting drowsy and was about ready to drift off to sleep when Michael banged on my door.

I did not know it was Michael, of course, and I sat up, with my heart pounding, and called in a quavering voice, "Who's there?"

"You mean, 'Who goes there?' " Michael said.

"Oh, it's you." I breathed again and simmered back to normal. "What do you want?"

"I want to talk to you."

I got out of bed, moved the bureau and opened the door. "What are you doing here at this time of the morning?" I asked crossly.

"I'm a doctor."

"That's wishful thinking," I said and wondered if my eyes looked as much like a couple of crosses as they felt.

"My patients believe in me."

I said, "Really? Both of them?"

He fixed his eyes on my tousled hair and observed, "I've had a session with the police—and we ended in a deadlock. They say I went out with Frances and I say I didn't."

"You mean you're somewhat on the spot?"

He nodded, and a faint frown appeared on his forehead. "I went out with a blonde all right," he said after a moment, "but it wasn't Frances—it was her kid sister, Louise."

"Not so much of a kid at that," I suggested.

"She's as pretty as Frances was," he said, looking at me but not really seeing me, "and very much like her. The police are going to interview her in the morning."

"It's the most interesting little tidbit I've heard for weeks," I said acidly. "I'm glad you woke me at four in the morning to tell me—I couldn't have waited."

His blue eyes refocused on my face, and he laughed at me. "Get into a housecoat or a Mother Hubbard or something, Jessie, and come on out to the solarium. Vera's getting some coffee for us."

I said, "My God! She'll have it all over the place."

"The coffee?"

"Don't be a silly ass," I said impatiently. "You know what I mean—and you know what Vera is."

"I fixed her," he said airily. "I told her we were making a study of your unusual mentality and I wanted to make notes on it when it and you were at low ebb—i.e., the early hours of the morning."

"You picked the right time," I said bitterly. "I'm at rock bottom. And you've confirmed a suspicion that has been growing in Vera all night—i.e., that I am heading straight for the state asylum."

He said that that was fine and would certainly stop Vera from spreading gossip about us and went off to the solarium to wait for me. I got into a negligee, brushed my hair and tried to fix up my face a bit. I had nearly finished when Michael came back and told me, for God's sake, to hurry up, because he needed to get some sleep.

I went out into the hall just as Vera appeared with the coffee. Her lips were folded into a narrow line, and her eyes were cold and disapproving.

I sidled up to her and whispered, "It's a shame—when you have so much to do already."

She blossomed out like a flower and would have told me about what she had to do already, but Michael cut her short and sent her off.

We sat down with the coffee between us, and Michael observed, "Nice costume—but you ought to wear a boudoir cap."

"Very comical," I said politely. "Is there any other little thing you wanted to get cleared up before I go back to bed?"

"I had to take this opportunity to talk to you," he explained. "I don't get much chance in the daytime—and I knew you wouldn't be sleeping anyway."

I said, "No, no—of course not. I always have morning tea at four o'clock."

"All right—now listen. In the first place, I want you to be very careful. I don't know what's going on around here—but there's something. And those Bakers are behaving in a very peculiar fashion. I think you ought to keep away from them—don't get mixed up with them in any way."

"How can I help it?" I asked impatiently. "They surround me in here."

"Stay with your aunt during the day and come back here only to sleep."

I laughed thinly. "How long do you think I'd keep my sanity? Have you ever tried sitting with my aunt Isabelle all day?"

"I don't believe you realize how serious this is, Jessie," he said slowly, and his eyes were very blue and very grave. "You don't want to be mixed up in a murder."

I said, "No," and absently stirred my coffee. "Don't they know who did it yet? Or—or why?"

"If they know anything at all," Michael said, turning his cigarette in his long, immaculate fingers, "they haven't confided in me. But I wish I knew—" He shook his head, as though he wanted to dispose of some troublesome thought, and added, "Anyway, I wish you'd keep away from the Bakers. I'm going to try and get your aunt to leave, and then you'll be out of the mess."

"I don't think I'll have any trouble. The police questioned me, and I told them all I knew about it, and they haven't bothered me since."

He nodded, but his eyes were still troubled. He was silent for a moment, and then he abruptly killed his cigarette and said, "Well, we'll leave that and get to the other thing."

I took a cigarette for myself—although my mouth felt like the bottom of a bird cage and I didn't really want one. I said, "Oh, so there's something else."

"Of course. About this marriage, as arranged by your aunt—naturally, we can't do it."

I felt as though he had slapped my face. While my mind whirled around, wondering if he thought that I had put my aunt up to the whole thing, I was conscious of being glad that I did not blush easily.

I managed to say casually, "That's a pity. I've crocheted two antimacassars and sent to Grand Rapids for a catalogue."

He ran a hand through his hair and said abstractedly, "You see, I use what I make out of your aunt for my research."

"Oh," I said. "Research. That's very noble."

He frowned and lit another cigarette.

"When you get more prosperous you won't have time for research. It's deep waters, anyway, and you ought to leave it to the boys with brains."

"To hell with being prosperous," he said, half to himself, "if it means giving up my research."

"What did you do with that check Aunt Isabelle gave you?" I asked suddenly. "Order a dozen-and-a-half guinea pigs?"

"I didn't do a damn thing with it," he said indignantly. "I even bought your ring out of my own pocket."

"I hope it didn't mean that you had to go without your lunch," I said politely.

"Listen, Jessie, I don't want to lose your aunt's custom right now. If you'll only stick with me for a few months and humor her about our engagement I'd appreciate it. After that I'll return the ring money, turn you down and never darken your aunt's door again—probably by request. You'll be left in high favor with her."

"I'll be left all right," I said coldly.

"What do you mean?"

"Girls who get jilted are apt to lose face."

He said peevishly, "Oh, talk sense."

"Further," I went on calmly, "my supposed engagement to you for several months is going to throw a large monkeywrench in among the dates I should otherwise have with the one or two other gents I happen to know."

He sat for a moment, frowning at the floor and saying nothing. Then he stood up abruptly. "Damn your aunt!" he said. "Anyway, I'm not breaking the engagement right now."

"Neither am I," I said furiously. "And what's more, I'm going to tell Aunt Isabelle that I'll be ready to marry you next week."

"You must please yourself, of course." I could see that he was quite as angry as I was. "But remember—if you go to your aunt with any such suggestion I'll go through with it." He turned on his heel and left.

I knew that he meant what he said, and I pictured him squaring his shoulders and gritting his teeth, preparatory to going through the ordeal.

I got up and walked out of the solarium in a red haze of pure fury. Michael didn't give a damn about me—never had, never would—and yet he wanted to tie me up so that he could get more money out of Aunt Isabelle!

The dawn had broken, and I was so completely concerned with Michael and his general duplicity that I flounced straight into my old room without noticing my mistake. The fact that the bed was made up did not penetrate my anger either—but when I threw myself down on it and heard the loud squeak of the springs I came to with a shock that brought me to a sitting position. My eyes dropped to the floor between the two beds—and I saw a white hospital shoe. There was a foot in it— with a leg disappearing under the other bed.

CHAPTER NINETEEN

I DON'T BELIEVE I moved for a full minute. I felt paralyzed, and my voice seemed to have gone. I managed to get off the bed at last, and I sent a wild glance around the room. I realized my mistake then, and I lurched toward the door and fell heavily against it. I clawed at the handle and with failing strength pulled the door wide enough for my body to slip through.

As soon as I got into the hall my voice came back to me, and I screamed shrilly. I presently found myself at the door leading into the main hall, without knowing how I had got there. I screamed again— and then the floor rose up and hit me.

I was vaguely conscious of footsteps and voices, and after a while my vision cleared and I recognized Vera and Michael and, oddly, Trevis and Gregg.

Michael lifted me from the floor and carried me to my bed, and Vera immediately began to slap my hands and wrists about in a very irritating fashion. The pallid, rather dreamlike faces of Trevis and Gregg remained framed in the doorway.

I remember telling Vera, fretfully, to leave me alone, and then I whispered fearfully, "Did you see her?"

Vera stepped back, and Michael made an abrupt movement of some sort and said sharply, "Who? Where?"

"It's Frances," I said and began to cry. "She's still there—in the next room."

Vera gave a little shriek, and I could see Trevis and Gregg staring at me—their eyes seemed enormous somehow. Michael straightened up and, after looking at me steadily for a moment, turned and hurried out of the room. Vera followed him, and Trevis and Gregg disappeared behind them.

I could not stay there alone. I got to my feet unsteadily and made my way to the door. My head was spinning, but I managed to keep going, with the help of the wall, and got to the door of the next room just as Michael and Trevis were putting a still, whiteclad figure onto one of the beds. I caught a glimpse of blonde, blood-soaked hair—and then Vera saw me. She hurried over and bullied me back to my room and made me lie down. But her face was gray and her hands shaking.

"It's Olive Parsons," she said in a sick voice. "The same way. I'm not going to stay on this floor. I'm going."

I looked at her and felt peal after peal of shrill laughter bubbling behind a thin veil of control.

"Don't worry, stupid," I said loudly, "they won't touch you. You're not blonde, you see. You have to be blonde to qualify."

She stared at me and said with a noticeable quaver, "What are you talking about? Pull yourself together and be quiet!"

I felt the horrid desire to laugh die away and I drew a couple of long breaths. Vera sat down heavily on the side of my bed and put an unsteady hand to her head. Her cap was hanging over one ear.

"When did the two Bakers come in?" I asked after a moment.

She gave her head a little shake and dropped her hand into her lap. "I don't know—I was having trouble with thirty-two. I had just come back to the desk when Doctor Rand came along and asked for the coffee. When I came back from the guest suite thirty-two had his light on again, and I had to go."

"You didn't see Olive come up here then?"

She shivered and said, "No, I didn't."

"Did you see anyone go into the guest suite?"

She shook her head. "No—but I've hardly been at the desk for the last two hours."

She lapsed into silence and stared at the wall, and I looked out the window and tried vainly to interest myself in the fact that it was going to be a nice day. My mind returned persistently and stubbornly to Olive Parsons—murdered like Frances—and, like Frances, stuffed under the bed in that next room.

After a while I became aware of people out in the hall—footsteps going back and forth and a subdued murmur of voices. I listened apathetically for a time, and then Michael came in.

He peremptorily ordered Vera back to her post, and she rose immediately, but as she left the room she announced, over her shoulder, that she had spent her last night on the sixth floor.

Michael sat on the end of my bed and asked me what had happened, and I told him the whole thing.

He seemed far from satisfied. "But how could you have gone into the wrong room? I don't understand it. You were so scared even in your own room that you had to pull a bureau in front of the door—and yet you walk straight into the other room without noticing the difference, plunk down on the bed, although it was made up—"

"I did not plunk down on the bed," I said coldly. "I lay down on it."

"And still you don't notice anything or know where you are."

I hated to explain the thing to him fully—but I did not want him to think that I was either an imbecile or a liar. I said reluctantly, "It was your fault, if you must know. I was in a furious temper, and my mind kept going over and over everything that you had said. I wasn't thinking at all of what I was doing—and I wasn't scared any more—I was just angry."

He thought that over for a while and then he said slowly, "I'm sorry—I suppose you're right. My work means so damned much to me that it comes before anything else. You're probably more interested in your own affairs."

"How did you guess it?" I asked, furious all over again. "Somebody must have told you."

There was a thump on the door, and William Forrest stuck his head into the room. He said curtly, "What are you doing in here, Doctor Rand?"

"I was releasing the floor nurse to her duties," Michael said smoothly. "And Miss Warren is hysterical and cannot be left alone."

I was smoking a cigarette by that time, with one arm folded comfortably behind my head and my ankles crossed.

Mr. Forrest gave me an appraising stare with a pair of cold gray eyes and said to Michael, "Will you leave me alone with Miss Warren, please? I want to question her."

Michael shrugged and rose to his feet, and the official added a request that he would kindly wait in the solarium as he had been asked to do in the first place.

When Michael had gone William Forrest started in on me—quite pleasantly and considerately. He prefaced it with some remarks about the brutal murder of two blonde nurses.

"Then Olive? She was murdered too?" I stammered.

He nodded and asked, "Did you know her?"

"Why, yes. Not intimately, of course—but I know lots of the nurses by their first names." I told him all about Aunt Isabelle, by way of explanation.

He was very interested in Aunt Isabelle, and he asked so many questions about her that I began to have an uneasy feeling that he suspected her.

He left her after a while, however, and made me go over the entire evening for him—and anything else that might have happened since Frances' death. I even told him about Sheila's Thing. After that, to my horror, I found myself telling him all about how we had lost Aunt Isabelle.

He showed an intense interest in that, and the only explanation that I could offer was that she was searching for Edith and me. I could see by the look in his chilly gray eyes that I had practically put my aunt behind bars.

I made a feeble effort then to clear Aunt Isabelle's good name, but he stood up abruptly and changed the subject. "As far as you know, then, the black wallet has not been found by any of those who seem to be looking for it?"

"That's right," I said, still thinking of my poor aunt.

"Well, thank you very much. I'll be back later in the day. You'll be here where I can find you?"

"Oh yes," I said wearily.

He hesitated at the door. "Can you think of anything that might have been used as a weapon?"

I shook my head, and he went out.

"Weapon," my brain repeated tiredly. Weapon! Those handles that were used to wind the beds up—the two that I had seen lying on the floor—one in Mr Baker's room and the other here in my own room!

I got up slowly and walked around the end of the beds. I went past the handle that had been lying on the floor and looked first at the other one.

The end was sticky with blood, and there were two blonde hairs clinging to it.

CHAPTER TWENTY

I DROPPED the thing onto the floor and ran out of the room. I went to the solarium, but neither Forrest nor Michael was there, and the place seemed to be deserted.

I went out into the main corridor and found Vera at the desk. "Where's that man, Forrest?" I gasped.

"He's gone," she said indifferently. "They've all gone." She shivered and added, "They took her—Olive—away some time ago. And when I go off duty here I am not coming back—ever."

I told her we'd all miss her and then asked her to phone downstairs and get them to contact Forrest, because I had something to tell him.

She put the message through and wanted to know immediately afterward what it was I had to tell Forrest.

I explained, and she gasped once or twice. "Where is it?" she asked, exhibiting all the signs of morbid curiosity.

I told her to go and see for herself, and she went finally—probably because it was light by that time.

Edith came up the hall, yawning all the way. She blinked at me and asked, "What are you doing out of bed at this hour? And where's Vera-and Olive? The old man needs some attention, and Olive isn't there."

I sat down at the desk heavily and twisted my hands together to keep them from shaking. "Didn't you hear it?" I asked after a moment. "All the racket?"

She stared at me and repeated, "Racket?"

I told her then—hating the necessity for having to go over it all again—and I saw her face go gray.

She steadied herself with one hand on the edge of the desk and said in a low voice, "My God! I'm going to get your aunt out of here today."

"I hope you succeed," I said wearily.

"If I don't," she muttered, "I'll cut my throat before someone does it for me." She turned away. "I'll go and fix Mr. Baker up, I guess."

I just sat there for a while—shaking and telling myself, at intervals, to snap out of it.

Footsteps on the stairway beside the elevator materialized into William Forrest and Michael—deep in conversation.

I hailed them hysterically and jabbered out an explanation about the handle, and they turned and made for the guest suite. Forrest paused and said something to Michael, who shrugged and returned to the desk.

"He doesn't want me," he said, sitting down and pulling out a cigarette.

I was afraid to try and answer him for fear I'd start screaming instead, so I sat quietly and listened to my teeth banging together.

I was conscious after a while of Michael's blue eyes on my face. He said quietly, "I'm going to give you something to make you sleep."

"I'm afraid to go to sleep," I said through my teeth. "It isn't safe."

He exhaled smoke through his nostrils and closed his eyes for a moment, as though he were tired. "I'll go and get Lenore, if you like, and let you go home."

I shook my head. "She wouldn't come. But I'm going to speak to Aunt Isabelle and try to get her to go home. If she refuses I'll go anyway."

He nodded. "Only you must get some sleep in the meantime. You'll be safe enough in your room now. Forrest and his gang will be milling around in there all day, most probably."

I said, "All right," and decided that I would sleep until ten or eleven and then get up and leave the place forever.

Vera came back at that point, muttering angrily to herself. "I don't care," she said when she saw us, "if he is a city official. He has no right to call me names."

"None whatever," Michael agreed. "What name did he call you?"

"It was behind my back," Vera admitted. "He didn't know I was listening—and he called me an interfering old witch."

"Witch?" Michael repeated, smiling faintly.

She nodded innocently and made a vexed sound with her tongue.

Michael allowed the smile to die away and then spoke to her in a businesslike undertone. She trotted off and presently returned with a paper cup, which contained a pill of some sort, and a glass of water. She offered them to me and managed to convey, without saying anything, that her need for the drug was greater than mine.

I swallowed the thing and went straight off to my room. I barely glanced at the spot where the handle had been lying, for I had made up my mind to put the whole thing away from me. I got into bed and went out like a light.

Much later I struggled up through deep black layers of sleep to the sound of a persistent knocking on the door. I got out of bed, pulled on a negligee and opened the door with drowsiness still floating around me like a gray fog.

Trevis stood there, smiling at me. "I hated to wake you—but your aunt's nurse told me to—and your supper is in there."

I pushed at the hair that was sticking damply to my forehead and said, "My God! What time is it?"

"Twenty past six. Don't wait to dress or the food will be cold. And that thing you have on is very charming."

My brain cleared completely, and I glanced down at the trailing white chiffon and laughed. "I won't dress—but I must powder my nose."

Trevis said, "I wouldn't argue against the inevitable—I'll wait for you in the solarium," and went off.

I turned back into the room and realized that I was feeling much better. I repaired my face and hair, whistling softly, and then made my way to the solarium.

Sheila and Gregg were seated at a small table and had started their meal. Trevis' tray and mine were on another table close by, and Trevis, who had been standing at one of the windows, came over and seated me, while Gregg half rose, with a mumbled good evening.

Sheila nodded briefly. She seemed to be quite herself again, and I wondered if the two men knew about her drunk of the previous night.

There wasn't anything very sparkling in the way of conversation. Trevis made an obvious effort to be pleasant, while Sheila and Gregg made none at all. They finished the meal in silence and then went off to their room. Miss Gould appeared shortly after they had left and announced briefly that my aunt wanted me.

"I'll walk down with you," Trevis said, "and look in on my uncle."

We went out into the main corridor, and my eyebrows flew up as I saw that Vera was just coming on. "I thought you were never coming here again," I called to her.

"And I thought you were going home this morning," she snapped back.

"Both wrong," I said and passed on, but I saw her little black eyes taking in every detail of the white chiffon negligee.

Mr. Baker's door was closed, but Trevis opened it quietly, nodded to me and slipped inside. Miss Gould left me at Aunt Isabelle's door and said she'd be right outside, if we wanted her.

I went in and Aunt Isabelle looked me up and down.

"Does your mother allow you to wear that thing in public?"

"Not on Broadway," I said, "or in the subway. But—"

"Don't you exercise your sarcasm on me, my good girl," said Aunt Isabelle. "I know as well as the next one that you're walking around practically in your nightgown in order to give those Baker boys a thrill."

"Aunt Isabelle!"

"Hush your silly chatter," she said peremptorily. "I want to hear all about last night."

I settled myself in the armchair and told her the whole tale from start to finish.

She considered it for a while, frowning thoughtfully. "Every time I hear the story," she said presently, "it changes. I can't seem to get it down exactly. Now nobody told me about your seeing those handles lying on the floor."

"I guess nobody knew," I explained. "I told Forrest—and then only after I had found the—the horrid one."

She said, "Hum. Those handles. The weapon, in each case."

I shuddered and said desperately, "It's ghastly, Aunt Isabelle. Can't we go home?"

"Don't talk nonsense," she said irritably. "You know very well that I'm in no condition to be moved."

I sighed, and she went on after a moment, "There must be another one somewhere."

"Another what?" I asked, not really caring.

"Bloodstained handle, of course."

I said, "Oh," and thought it over. "But the same one might have been used in both cases."

"Possible," said Aunt Isabelle. "But on the whole, I think improbable."

I shrugged and wished that she would stop talking about it.

"Look at mine," she said suddenly.

"Your what?"

"Bed handle!" she yelled. "Why don't you listen?"

I went to the end of the bed and pulled the thing out and looked at it—but it was quite clean.

"All right," she said. "Now go and look in Mr. Baker's room."

"I can't. Trevis is in there."

"Who?"

"Trevis Baker. The old man's nephew."

"Trevis," she said. "Getting pretty familiar, aren't you? You shouldn't be calling a man by his first name when you're engaged to another."

"No?"

"No," she said firmly. "And things like that bit of white drip should be reserved for your husband. Now go on into Mr. Baker's room and look at that handle—and then come straight back."

"But I can't," I protested. "Trevis and the nurse are both there."

"Then go back to your own room and look at the handle in the other bed."

I said, "Listen, Aunt Isabelle. Surely you realize that the police must have done that long ago. Good heavens, it's a murder investigation."

"Thanks for telling me," she said dryly. "I didn't know—I thought the girls had died of old age. And as for the police—why should they bother being thorough? It's only the taxpayers' money."

I gave it up, heaved myself out of the armchair and went along to my room.

But I did not look at the handle right away. When I switched on the light a flash of blue fire from the bureau caught my eye, and the next minute I was holding in my hand a diamond ring—not Michael's two-bit variety, but the real thing—large and beautiful and obviously valuable.

CHAPTER TWENTY-ONE

I TURNED the ring over in my hands curiously. I knew it was not modern. The diamonds had an old-fashioned setting of yellow gold, but it was unobtrusive, and the stones, arranged in a cluster, were large and of good quality. I slipped it onto my finger and turned my hand this way and that, admiring the expensive flash that it gave out.

But who could have left a valuable ring on my bureau—and why? I decided at last to give it to Vera and tell her to send it down to the office.

I remembered then why I had come, and I gingerly drew the handle from the other bed. It was quite clean, and I heaved a sigh of relief and put it back.

I went out into the main corridor, but Vera was not at the desk, so I continued down the hall with the ring still on my finger.

Mr. Baker's door was open, and a glance showed me that Trevis was gone. Miss Kane, busy at the basin, looked up, and I inquired after her patient. She dried her hands and came to the door. "He's fair, I guess," she said, settling her glasses.

"I heard yesterday that he was dying."

She shrugged and said, "I wouldn't know."

It seemed to me that she wouldn't know much of anything anyway, so I passed on to my aunt's room.

Miss Gould was there in tears.

"Now, what?" I asked.

"That girl!" said Aunt Isabelle. "She weeps about everything. I merely told her that she'd never get a husband, looking as drab as she does. I was trying to help—that's all. As I see it she ought to glamour herself up a bit."

"Why didn't you glamour yourself up a bit when you were young?" Miss Gould sobbed with unexpected fire.

"I didn't need glamour," said Aunt Isabelle tartly. "I had brains and money. Now get out. I want to talk to Jessie."

Miss Gould flung her head up and made for the door, and just before she disappeared Aunt Isabelle called after her, "You needn't think—just because I never married—that I didn't have offers either."

Miss Gould allowed the door to close behind her without further comment, and my aunt settled herself on her pillows and gave me a sharp look. "Did you find it?"

"No."

"Where did you look?" she asked crossly.

"Where you told me. The other bed in my room."

She pursed her lips and said after a moment, "What about the other room?"

"What other room?"

"The room you slept in at first," she snapped impatiently.

I said firmly, "Nothing would induce me to go into that room—especially at night."

"The women had more enterprise in my day," she said scornfully.

"I don't care what they had. I'm moving out of here tomorrow—and I'd advise you to do the same."

"Michael would never allow me to be moved," she said, trying to look pathetic, "and so I'll have to stay, whatever happens. As far as you're concerned, of course, you can go at any time and leave me to face it alone."

She lay quietly for a while, probably trying to squeeze out a tear—and then she absentmindedly lit a cigar and spoiled the effect.

Unexpectedly Edith walked in, and my aunt eyed her narrowly. "What are you doing here at this time?"

"The police wanted to question me on a few points," she explained, "so I had my dinner when they had finished with me and came on around."

"Send Miss Gould home then," said Aunt Isabelle.

"Why should I?" Edith asked with spirit. "I'm only visiting until eleven o'clock."

My aunt ignored this and asked alertly, "What did you learn from the police?"

"Nothing. I've told you at least three times all I know about it—and when the police call you for questioning they don't tell—they ask."

"Keep your temper," said my aunt, "and hold your tongue." She was silent for a while and then she said thoughtfully, "It's that black wallet. If we could only find it we'd probably know everything."

"Why?" Edith asked flatly.

"Don't be stupid. There must be *something* in the wallet—otherwise why are they all searching for it so frantically?"

Edith shrugged. "If you ask me, those Bakers are all cracked."

"I didn't ask you," said Aunt Isabelle, "but I admit your ability to recognize your own kind." She thought that was pretty good and lay chuckling over it for some time, while Edith studied her nails, which badly needed repainting.

"The three of them," Edith said after a while, "hanging around, waiting for the old man to die, so that they can get his money. And I'll bet he leaves it elsewhere."

"You're living in a glass house to be throwing stones," my aunt said significantly.

Edith said, "Well—if you don't have me down in your will for about ten thousand I think it's pretty darned mean of you. But, as far as that goes, I don't expect to outlive you."

"No," said my aunt acidly, "you'll die of fatty degeneration of the heart."

Edith made no comment, and I rested my head against the back of the chair and drowsed comfortably with my eyes half closed.

There was a short silence while my aunt blew smoke rings at the ceiling and appeared to meditate. Then she said casually, "I'm offering a prize of twenty-five dollars to whichever of you finds that other handle."

I started up out of my chair, and Edith shouted, "What other handle?"

I was already on my way out of the room while Aunt Isabelle explained briefly. "Also," she added, raising her voice so that I could hear, "a bonus of fifty dollars for whoever produces the black wallet."

Edith was close at my heels, and we raced to the guest suite. Vera called out, "Shh," several times as we passed the desk.

With seventy-five dollars looming up before me I closed my mind to my fears and made straight for that terrible room where the two girls had been found. Edith was right with me, and we each pulled a handle out of one of the beds—but they were both clean. We banged them back and made a feverish search for the black wallet, but we didn't find it.

"Phew!" Edith said as we came out. "That's the worst over anyway."

We searched the solarium, with no success, and then put our ears against the door of the Gregg Bakers' room. We could hear them inside, apparently having a low-voiced argument—but although we held our breaths and strained our ears we could not make out one word, so we moved on to Trevis' room. All was quiet there, so we knocked, but there was no response. We pushed the door open, and Edith whispered, "You go in. It won't matter if you get caught, but I'd get into trouble."

"What about the seventy-five dollars?" I asked.

"No use cutting each other's throats," she said practically. "We'll organize this search together and divide the money."

I nodded, slipped into the room and switched on the light. The room was neat and impersonal. The handles in both beds were clean, and my hasty search for the wallet was unproductive. I went out again with a little sigh of relief.

Edith whispered that the Gregg Bakers were still arguing.

"Where can we search now?" I asked.

"How about the empty rooms in my wing? You never know."

We hurried out and down the hall, but it was a washout. We did not find what we were looking for, and Vera caught on to what we were doing after a while and came down to tell us we couldn't do it. We paid no attention to her, and she followed us around, making threats.

When we had finished Edith said she'd take care of old Mr. Baker's room when she got a chance and leave the Gregg Bakers' room to me. I agreed, and she returned to Aunt Isabelle, while I went along to the solarium.

I stretched out on the chaise longue with a cigarette and flapped my ears in the direction of the Gregg Bakers' room, but the argument seemed to have stopped.

Sheila came out after a while. She was frowning and looked thoroughly cross. She sat down close beside me and pulled out a cigarette, which she tapped viciously on the arm of her chair. I saw her eyes, which had been stormy and sullen, focus sharply on my hand. I glanced down, and at the same time she said in a voice of cold fury, "What are you doing with that ring on your finger?"

CHAPTER TWENTY-TWO

INVOLUNTARILY I closed my fingers. "I forgot about it," I said hastily. "I must give it to Vera."

I stood up, but Sheila barred my way. "What do you mean? Who's Vera? That ring belongs to Mr. Baker."

I said, "Does it? I found it on the bureau in my room."

She gave me a rather nasty look of unbelief and held out her hand. "You had better give it to me."

"I think I ought to give it to the authorities," I said doubtfully. "It was lying on my bureau—and I don't want to get into any trouble over it."

"Oh, for heaven's sake, give it to me," she said impatiently. "Tell the authorities if you want to—but give me the ring."

I handed it over reluctantly, and she snatched it and slipped it onto her finger. She turned away, and I went on out to find Vera, because I wanted to tell her about it and thus have it on record that my intentions were honest.

Vera was nowhere to be seen, of course—which was usual when I wanted her, and while I stood at the desk, hesitating, William Forrest stepped out of the elevator.

I hailed him, with a sigh of relief, and told him all about the ring, and he turned toward the guest suite immediately. I followed him and told him on the way of the search Edith and I had made for the black wallet. Delicacy prevented me from mentioning the fifty-dollar prize offered by my Aunt Isabelle.

He gave me a faint grin and said, "You keep your beautiful red head out of this business, gal."

I smiled and said meekly, "Yes sir."

Sheila was reading a magazine in the solarium. She glanced up at us, and Forrest said directly, "Will you show me the ring that you just obtained from Miss Warren, Mrs. Baker?"

She shot me a venomous look and extended her hand.

"Will you take it off, please," Forrest said courteously, "so that I can examine it?"

She removed it from her finger sulkily and tossed it into the palm of his hand. "It belongs to Mr. Baker," she said haughtily, "so naturally I asked for it when I saw Miss Warren wearing it."

"Naturally," said Forrest, his voice faintly colored with sarcasm.

He looked the thing over carefully and murmured, " 'From Ames to Mary.' Who was Mary?" he asked, glancing at Sheila.

"Mr. Baker's wife," she replied shortly.

"She died some time ago?"

"Fifteen years ago," Sheila said and lit a fresh cigarette.

"And he did not marry again?"

"No."

Forrest closed his hand over the ring. "Have you any idea, Mrs. Baker, how this ring could have been left on Miss Warren's bureau?"

Sheila flicked her eyes at me and said, "None whatever."

"Do you know, then, where Mr. Baker usually kept it?"

"He—kept it on him."

"In one of his pockets?"

She tapped her cigarette over the ashtray and hesitated. "Well—no," she said finally.

"In the black wallet then?"

She raised her lashes in a swift upward glance, and her eyes had a startled look. "Why—yes—I think so," she said after a moment.

"Just one thing more," Forrest said. "Have you, or has anyone else, to your knowledge, found that wallet yet?"

She twisted the cigarette in her fingers until it was partially mangled and said slowly, "Not that I know of."

"And yet this ring probably came from the wallet?" She nodded.

"Thank you very much, Mrs. Baker," he said with a slight bow—and departed forthwith. I watched him go down the hall and was not at all surprised when he made a left turn into my room.

Sheila said furiously, "He has no right to keep that ring."

"Maybe he wants it as evidence. You'll get it back eventually."

She frowned and took up her magazine again, and I wandered down the hall and stood at the door of my room. William Forrest was making a methodical search of the place.

He looked up and saw me after a while and asked pleasantly, "Do you mind?"

I said, "Not at all," and continued to watch. But he did not unearth anything.

"You say you searched the other rooms?" he asked, mopping at his damp face with his handkerchief.

I nodded. "All but the Gregg Bakers', Mr. Baker's—and now that I come to think of it, my Aunt Isabelle's."

He put the handkerchief away. "We did them all before, of course—but now that this ring has turned up I feel that I should do it again. The wallet might have been returned in the meantime."

"Do you think somebody took it?" I asked curiously.

He said he didn't know and made for the solarium again.

Sheila was still reading her magazine, and Forrest asked if he might search her room. She shrugged and said it made no difference to her, but she'd have to wake her husband.

Forrest didn't try to stop her, and she went in rather ungraciously and apparently dragged Gregg out of a sound sleep. He came out, wrapped up untidily in a silk dressing gown, blinking and looking decidedly annoyed. I felt for him a bit, knowing, as I did, that he had been up most of the night before. He slumped into one of the wicker chairs in the solarium and pulled out a crumpled package of cigarettes.

Sheila stood at the door and watched, but I went in and pulled out the two bed handles and looked at them—because I thought Forrest wasn't going to do it. They were both clean.

He glanced at me. "You don't miss much, redhead, do you?" he asked, laughing a little.

I replaced the handles and retreated to the door.

When he had finished he left the room, with a nod to Sheila, and went down the corridor and out of the guest suite. I followed him.

He looked at me once and said, "If ever you want a job as a tail—"

I blushed and dropped back a foot, but he grinned at me and said, "Well, tail on."

We passed Vera, who made various signs to me, but I could not make them out and I wouldn't stop, for fear of losing Forrest.

He passed Mr. Baker's room, knocked briefly on my aunt's door and went in. Miss Gould had gone, but Edith was there and so was Michael.

"May I search your room, Miss Daniel?" Forrest asked.

Aunt Isabelle said, "No," at once, but he spoiled her fun by retreating without argument, and she had to call him back.

"I was never one to block the course of justice," she said by way of excuse. "You may search if you wish." She pulled her purse out from under the pillow, clutched it tightly in her two hands and prepared to watch.

William Forrest searched the room quickly and efficiently, found nothing and bowed himself out. I did not follow him this time—probably because of Michael. But he had the nerve to pop his head back into the room and say, "Oh, there you are. I had a feeling that something was missing."

He disappeared again, and Michael said lazily, "Joke?"

"Not for your amusement," I said, arranging myself in the armchair. "Strictly between the law and me."

Aunt Isabelle made an impatient movement that was designed to draw the general attention to herself. "Get out, Edith," she said. "I want to talk to these two alone—and I don't often get a chance."

Edith retired and closed the door behind her—but I knew perfectly well that she would stay directly outside, with her ear glued to the crack.

Michael frowned and studied his shoe.

Aunt Isabelle shifted the purse on her lap and continued to clutch it with both hands. "Now I want to know what plans you young people have made."

Michael was still absorbed in his shoe, so I said, "Plans, Aunt Isabelle?"

"When do you intend to get married?" she snapped.

"Next week," I said promptly and added, "On Tuesday."

She looked at me with slightly narrowed eyes and asked, "Why Tuesday?"

"Oh—I don't know," I said idiotically. "Michael goes to church on Sunday—and Monday's washday—"

"That will do!" she said coldly. "As for Tuesday—it's too soon."

"Well, how about Wednesday?"

"You watch your tongue with me, girl, or you'll be sorry," she barked.

I sat up and threw back my shoulders. "I am serious. When the time comes I shall go through with it."

Michael abandoned his shoe and began to play around with something in his vest pocket that was either a thermometer or a fountain pen. "You can stop clowning, Jessie," he said slowly. "I'll draw out." He raised his head and looked at Aunt Isabelle. "I'm sorry to disappoint you, Miss Daniel—but Jessie and I have decided not to marry after all."

I could see fury leap and sparkle in her eyes, but for a moment she said nothing. When she did speak her voice was surprisingly quiet. "We'll discuss it in the morning, Michael. Go on home now and try to get some well-earned rest."

He said good night, looking a bit surprised, and winked at me on his way out.

I waited for the torrent of abuse, and it started immediately—*sotto voce* at first, so that Michael would not hear—but working, at last, into a full, strong bass. Edith came back in the middle of it to get in on the fun.

Aunt Isabelle put the entire blame on me and accused me of inciting Michael to make the break.

I did not waste breath on denials—I simply sat there and admired the storm.

Finally, in emphasizing a point, she banged her purse down onto her knee. She let out a howl of pain, and at the same time the purse flew open and a cascade of small objects poured onto the bedspread and from there to the floor. I stooped to recover them and felt my eyes pop. One of the things was a small black leather wallet, engraved with a gilt B.

CHAPTER TWENTY-THREE

I MADE a dive for the wallet, and at the same time Aunt Isabelle shouted, "Give that back to me at once!"

I looked at the thing, and Edith came and peered over my shoulder.

"Where did you get it, Aunt Isabelle?" I asked.

"Give it to me," she yelled. "At once, do you hear?"

I backed away from the bed with my hands behind me. "The police are looking for it, and I ought to hand it over to them—or shall I tell them that you have it?"

She laughed grimly. "If you tell them I have it—I'll tell them where I found it."

"What do you mean? Where did you find it?"

"Wrapped up in that pair of green satin panties that I gave you for your birthday two years ago. And I don't believe you've ever worn them."

Diverted, I cast my mind back to the green satin pants and remembered that I had brought them to the hospital for the sole purpose of leaving them when I went home. Even Aunt Isabelle should have known that they were atrocious.

"I've been keeping them for my trousseau," I explained. "They're so unusual. But what do you mean by saying they were wrapped around the wallet?"

"Don't think you're fooling me," she said shortly. "You must have put the wallet there."

"I did nothing of the sort!" I snapped impatiently. "I have no idea how it came to be there. Anyway, I'm going to hand it over to the police."

"Why not the Bakers?" Edith suggested mildly. "After all, it belongs to them."

"Well—maybe. I'm going to give it to somebody."

"Then why not me?" Aunt Isabelle said reasonably. "Come on, Jessie—hand it back."

She was getting impatient and heading toward the explosion point, but I figured that I was in the doghouse anyway, and I wanted to examine the content at my leisure.

"I'm not going to give it to you," I said firmly. "If you haven't sense enough to keep out of jail yourself I'll do what I can to help."

I turned and left the room, holding the wallet firmly in my hand and trying to close my ears to the bellows that followed me.

I went straight into the empty room across the hall and switched on the light—and found that Edith was close at my heels.

"You're a prize snoop," I told her.

"What about you?"

"I'm just as bad—and someday we'll both get into trouble."

"For God's sake, hurry up and open the thing," she said. "I've got to get back and stop her infernal yelling. She'll wake up the bodies in the morgue."

I emptied the wallet and spread the contents on the counterpane of the bed. There was no money at all and apparently nothing of value. There was a collection of newspaper clippings—activities of the Baker family. I read an account of Mr. Baker's wedding, Mrs. Baker's obituary, the marriage of Sheila and Gregg, Trevis' golfing triumphs and a few other clippings about people I did not know. There were a few stamps and two pieces of paper. One was quite blank, and on the other, written in a cramped hand, were the words, "Please meet me on Tuesday."

We looked that over very carefully and examined it thoroughly, but the only deduction we were able to make was that it was not as old as most of the newspaper clippings.

"Seems pretty innocuous to have created such a furor," I said, disappointed. "I'll give it to the police and see if they can make anything out of it."

Edith yawned and made for the door. "I'll have to go and shut her up somehow. I wish to God I could just stuff a sponge in her mouth and be done with it." She hurried across the hall, and I replaced the things in the wallet and took it along to the desk.

Vera told me that William Forrest had gone, and after a moment's indecision I made up my mind to give the wallet straight to the Bakers.

I went along to the guest suite and found that it was in complete darkness. I felt my way to my room and turned the light on—and tried to ignore the fact that my knees were shaking. I mentally cursed the person who was always turning lights off in the guest suite—and remembered Sheila's Thing and tried frantically to think of something else.

It was just twelve o'clock, and the Bakers' rooms seemed to be in complete darkness. I did not want to go banging on their doors at that hour—although I knew that they were desperate to get their hands on the wallet—even to the point of Sheila throwing hysterics so that I would give it to her. I wondered why it could possibly be so important to them—when there wasn't really a damn thing in it.

I could not understand either why it had been wrapped up in those beastly green pants. Granted that Aunt Isabelle was telling the truth about it, the wallet could not have been there for long—since I had spent most of my time recently searching the entire sixth floor.

I began to feel a bit uncomfortable about the Bakers. I had found their ring on my bureau and been caught wearing it—and now I had their superimportant black wallet.

I shrugged the thought away, made up my mind to give the wallet to Forrest in the morning and went out into the main corridor again, because the darkness and silence was making my scalp prickle.

I sat down beside Vera at the desk and pulled out a cigarette.

She glanced at me and said crisply, "No smoking."

I struck a match and lit up and then searched absentmindedly for an ashtray. Vera ignored me and continued to punish her fountain pen, and at that moment an undergraduate pattered by, wearing a voluminous blue-and-white-striped dress and carrying a bedpan. The bedpan was decently covered with a white cloth.

I hailed her, and she threw a glance at Vera and then came to a stop and looked at me inquiringly. I asked her if she had a spare one that I could use for an ashtray. She looked at me helplessly and again at Vera—who sharply ordered her to get on about her business. I sighed and flicked ash onto the floor.

"Where were you about fifteen minutes ago?" Vera asked presently without looking up from her writing.

"I don't know. Why?"

"Mr. Trevis Baker was searching frantically for you."

"When?"

"I have just told you," she said, obviously praying for patience. "About fifteen minutes ago."

"What did he want?"

"You," she said, losing her temper despite her prayer. "Why don't you listen? Your aunt was making a most unnecessary and disgraceful noise, and he and the nurse went in to see what was wrong."

I said, "Oh—he was still down there then. He's been visiting down there all night."

"If you want to hear it you had better stop interrupting. My time is valuable. Apparently your aunt told Mr. Baker that you had found his wallet—and he came tearing up the hall and into the guest suite. He came flying out again almost right away and asked me where you had

gone. I told him I didn't know, so he went back into the guest suite and
stayed there for about five minutes. He came out again and went down
the hall to your aunt's room, and then he came back and went down in
the elevator, after asking me again if I had seen you."

I realized, of course, that I had been in the vacant room with Edith
while all this had been going on—and apparently Trevis had just missed
me. I didn't care much. I was getting a bit tired of the Bakers and their
intrigues, and I was more than ever determined to hand the wallet over
to Forrest in the morning.

I stood up. "Listen, Vera, if he comes back tell him I handed the
wallet straight over to the police and that I've gone to bed and don't
want to be disturbed. And wake me up as soon as Forrest comes—no
matter what time it is."

She nodded. "Very well. But tell me—what is in that wallet?"

"Nothing," I said and went off to the guest suite, determined to get
some sleep and to keep out of Trevis' way.

The light was still burning in my room, and I went in and looked
under the beds and in the bathroom. Everything seemed to be all right,
so I went back into the bedroom.

A nurse stood at the bureau, with her back to me. She was slender
and blonde, and I felt the perspiration spring out in my palms and on
my forehead, because I could have sworn that it was Frances Hoffman.

CHAPTER TWENTY-FOUR

SHE MUST HAVE HEARD me gasp, for she turned around and faced me—
and of course it wasn't Frances.

"Oh, Miss Warren," she said, "I'm Louise Hoffman—Frances' sister."

"You—you look very like her," I said feebly.

"Yes, I know." Her eyes filled with tears, and I tried to murmur
something comforting. We sat down on the bed, and I gave her a clean
handkerchief.

"I don't understand it," she said after a while. "Frances never had any enemies—everybody liked her. She was always laughing and having a good time, and she was nice to everyone."

I said slowly, "What happened about Miss Zimmerman's boyfriend? Wasn't he attracted to Frances?"

"Oh, that—sure." She raised her head, and the light glistened on her wet lashes. "He took a fancy to Frances and tried to date her up—but she never went out with him—not once. Miss Zimmerman quarreled with him about it, but she told Frances that she didn't blame her—and I heard her telling it with my own ears."

"It's queer," I said with a little sigh. "There just doesn't seem to be any reason why anyone should want to kill her."

"I've thought about it until I'm nearly crazy. I just had to talk to someone so I came to you. Frances used to tell me about you."

"What floor are you on?" I asked.

"Right here—Mr. Baker. I'm taking Olive's place."

I shivered and found myself wishing that she were a brunette—or that her work had been on any floor but the sixth.

"I had to take the job," Louise said, dabbing at her eyes. "I have to live—and I have to pay for Frances' funeral. We never saved any money, you know—we always spent the last nickel." She drew a long quivering breath. "I wish I could have gone away for a while."

"It's a shame. Haven't you some relative you could go and visit for a while?"

She shook her head. "They're all poor. Our parents died years ago, and Frances and I were the only children. The aunts and uncles and cousins are used to receiving help from us—not giving it"

"I'm sorry," I said. "It's hard on you. But I wish they hadn't put you on this floor. Anywhere else—"

"Oh well"—she began to repair her face—"it's a good job—aside from the association. And then, as I say, I need the money."

I watched her for a while in silence and then I asked, "Did you know Olive Parsons?"

"Yes—quite well."

"Did you like her?"

She shut her compact with a firm click. "No—not much. She was mean and greedy and wanted everything for herself."

"Then she could have had enemies?"

"Sure she could, plenty of them, only—" She broke off abruptly, frowning and staring into space.

"Only what?" I urged.

She gave her, head a little shake. "I don't know who her enemies were," she said.

I felt sure that she had thought of somebody, but I could not very well press it so I changed the subject. My eye had caught the small bottle of cheap perfume that I had found in the other room and that was still standing on the bureau.

I remembered that Louise had been at the bureau when I came out of the bathroom, so I asked her about it.

"Cheap stuff," she said promptly. "I wouldn't use it. But a lot of the girls bathe in that sort of stuff if the bottle is cute enough."

"Is that what you were looking at a little while ago?" I asked.

She shook her head. "I wasn't looking at anything. Just waiting for you."

"Do you know any of the girls who might be the owner?"

"Of that perfume, do you mean? Several of them—but nobody in particular."

"Well, who would be likely to come up here to the guest suite for a nap?"

Louise raised her eyebrows and said, "Hmm."

"I know someone came up last night and left that bottle," I explained. "You needn't worry about giving anyone away."

"They come up from the fifth floor sometimes," she admitted, "and snatch some sleep."

"Could you find the one who left the perfume for me?"

"Why—I don't know," she said doubtfully and with faint suspicion.

"I don't want to tell on her," I said hastily, "I want to return the perfume."

She relaxed visibly. "I guess I can run her to earth in that case." She stood up and smoothed her immaculate uniform. "I'd better get back to my patient—although he's due to sleep for a while yet."

She said good night and went off, and I continued to sit on the bed, thinking it all over.

Olive and Frances had looked pretty much alike, from the back view, and since it was likely that Olive had enemies I wondered whether Frances had been killed in mistake for her. And then, when the mistake was discovered, the murderer had killed Olive the following night.

Louise might have had some special grudge against Olive, of course—but, on the other hand, Olive might have been mean and greedy. Certainly I had no way of knowing. I decided to consult with Edith about it.

I stirred and glanced at the bureau and the doorhigh time to barricade myself in.

I stood up—and at the same time the door swung slowly inward.

CHAPTER TWENTY-FIVE

I THINK I must have expected Sheila's Thing to walk in—I know I was stiff with fear—but it was only Trevis. He appeared to be considerably startled when he saw me. "Oh—I beg your pardon," he stammered. "I—didn't you hear me knock?"

He hadn't knocked, and my expression must have told him that I knew it. He smiled suddenly and with all his charm. "You're almost never here, you know—and your door is usually open. I hope you'll forgive me."

"We live an informal life here," I said, smiling too.

He said pleasantly, but with a certain tenseness, "I heard that you had found my uncle's wallet."

"Oh yes," I said in some confusion. "Didn't Vera tell you—"

"She said that you had given it to the police. But I see that you still have it."

I glanced down at the wallet that was still tightly clutched in my hand. "Yes, I—"

"May I have it?" he asked.

I handed it over, because I did not see what else I could do about it.

He said, "Thanks," and slipped it into his pocket without looking at it.

"How's your uncle?" I asked inanely and for the sake of saying something.

"Just about the same," Trevis said cheerfully. He bowed himself out then, and I was left standing there.

I shrugged, moved the bureau in front of the door and prepared to go to bed.

I had just finished cleaning my face off when there was a bang on the door and Michael called, "Come on out. Vera's getting coffee."

I groaned, put my face back on and moved the bureau. Michael was smoking in the solarium.

"Don't you ever go home?" I asked crossly. "Or do you wait around for the ambulance to come in so you'll maybe catch some business?"

"I was not only at home," he said, eying my hair, "but tucked snugly in my bed. I came back on an emergency call."

I said, "Oh yes. The spaniel belonging to one of the ambulance drivers. I heard she was due to whelp."

"You'll have me in stitches," Michael said, lighting a cigarette. "The call was from your aunt. Edith put it through and said she'd been told to say that if I did not come at once I could consider myself dismissed from the case. I thought I'd already been dismissed so I came running."

"Give me a cigarette too," I said wearily. "What was the emergency? Had she lost a nickel?"

"Your aunt," said Michael, dropping his head onto the back of his chair and staring at the ceiling, "is a very fine woman."

"I know all about her," I said coldly.

He took his eyes from the ceiling and looked at me with a faint smile. "I'm going to marry you on Tuesday after all."

"Do tell!"

"And Aunt Isabelle is giving me fifty thousand dollars for a wedding present."

"What!" I yelled.

"I couldn't turn down fifty thousand dollars," he said reasonably.

"I can't believe it!" I gasped. "I can see her giving you a hundred dollars—but fifty thousand! Never! Not my aunt Isabelle."

"Do you think she intends to back out after the wedding?"

I shook my head. "No," I said slowly, "I've never known her to break her word in that way. But, on the other hand, I've never known her to offer anything approaching such a sum to anybody."

"She cares more for you than you think. She figures it won't be easy for you to snaffle a husband with that hair, so she's taking the time and money to arrange for your happiness."

Vera came in with the coffee, looking fit to be tied, and we were silent until she had left. I poured two cups and then sat back and said wonderingly, "I had no idea that I was worth all that to Aunt Isabelle." I took a swallow, burned my tongue and gave Michael a black look. "You needn't sit there with that look of beatitude. If you think you're going to make fifty thousand dollars out of me you're vastly mistaken."

"Don't be hasty, Jessie," he said reasonably. "Why spoil your entire future just to satisfy your pride at the moment? You'll be much better off as the wife of a rising young doctor, with fifty thousand dollars in his jeans, than if you go off and marry a penniless ne'er-do-well."

"Why should you suppose—"

"Never mind," he interrupted firmly. "We'll talk about it in the morning. Just now I'd like to see that wallet. Your aunt told me where she'd found it and how you got hold of it. Quite a long tale it was too."

"I can imagine," I said shortly. "Why should I hand it over to you?"

"Curiosity," he said mildly. "Also, I have an idea that it's dynamite, and I don't think you should keep it in your possession all night."

"You can relax then. Trevis has it."

He seemed quite upset by that and asked irritably, "Couldn't you have kept it?"

I told him how Trevis had got it, and he said, "Hmm. Didn't you look through it first?"

"Of course." I told him about the clippings and the stamps and the two pieces of paper. "So, you see, there really wasn't anything in it after all."

"Why all the frantic searching then?"

I shrugged, and at that moment Trevis appeared at the door.

"Miss Warren—are you sure there was nothing else in that wallet of my uncle's? It was only a slip of paper and it could have fallen out quite easily. I wonder—could you tell me where you found it, so that I can go and look?"

"I found it in my aunt's purse," I said, "and if you can figure out a way to look there I'll pin a medal on you. I'm quite sure, though, that nothing dropped out of it."

He thanked me, said good night to both of us and backed out.

"I'd like to hear Aunt Isabelle when he asks if he may search her purse," I said reflectively.

Michael grinned and stood up. "That fellow, Forrest, is going to be disappointed when he hears that the Bakers got the wallet before he did."

"I don't see why," I said as we moved out into the hall together. "It's pretty evident that the dynamite has been removed from the thing."

"I suppose so," he said and added, "Where's the damned light in this hall?"

"Away on vacation."

He came to a stop at my door and stood looking down at me. "You never say good night to your fiancee in a dark hall without embracing her."

"Carry on."

He kissed me, and I enjoyed it but I said, "Maybe a penniless ne'er-do-well would be better after all."

"You'll eat those words someday," he said darkly and went off.

I leaned against the wall and wished that I was not in love with him so that I could turn him down coldly, but I renewed my determination to telephone Lenore about bringing over some hats.

I was about to turn and go into my room, when I heard one of the windows in the solarium being cautiously raised.

CHAPTER TWENTY-SIX

I STOOD quite still and waited. My heart was thumping, but I think I was more excited and interested than frightened. I knew I could run out into the main corridor if anything appeared and started toward me—and I wanted to know who the intruder was.

Michael had turned the light off in the solarium. I could not see anything, and it was as still as death. Once, as I waited, I heard one of the chairs being moved—quietly and somehow stealthily—and after that it was silent again.

I began to have a nervous idea that the thing had got out of the solarium and was coming down the hall toward me, and my eyes ached from straining into the darkness.

Suddenly the Gregg Bakers' door was pulled open, and Sheila came out. I could not see her clearly, but she wore a light-colored negligee of some sort that had an almost phosphorescent glimmer. She turned and went toward the solarium, and I tried to call out and warn her, but my throat cracked and I could not utter a sound.

She got inside the door, and I could see the faint glow of her gown as she apparently groped for the light switch. I took a step forward, and at the same time she gave a low moan, backed into the hall and fell flat.

I banged on Trevis' door because it was nearest to me, but there was no response, and an instant later light flooded the Gregg Bakers' room and Gregg appeared at the door. Sheila lay in the bar of light that streamed out from behind him, and I heard him give a sharp exclamation of some sort.

I said wildly, "There's someone in the solarium—she's had some sort of a shock. Please go and look. I'll take care of her."

He did not want to go, but I made him, and in the meantime I slapped at Sheila's wrists and hoped it was the right treatment.

Gregg went into the solarium and switched on the light. He gave a brief look around and then came back.

"There's no one there," he said and lifted Sheila and carried her to her bed. "Will you get a nurse, please?" he asked over his shoulder.

I went out and got Vera, who was quite willing to come because she wanted to find out what had happened.

Sheila was crying when we got back. "It was that horrible thing again," she sobbed.

"But what was it?" Gregg asked wearily and with a touch of impatience.

"I don't know. It's dreadful."

"Surely you can tell us what it looks like," Gregg persisted.

"I've told you—I keep telling you—again and again and again—"

"Now, my dear," said Vera, beginning to bustle.

"I can't sleep," Sheila sobbed wildly. "I'm afraid—all the time. I wait for the door to open—"

"Put the bureau in front of it," I said practically.

But Sheila only moaned, and Vera crisply ordered me to leave.

I waited outside the door, and after a while Vera appeared, and it seemed to me that Gregg was almost pushing her out. I accompanied her back to the desk.

"I wouldn't be able to sleep," I said, "even with the bureau in front of the door."

"Then sit down for a while," Vera said almost chummily, "and tell me all about it."

I told her all about it and wound up by asking her if she knew where Trevis was.

She shook her head and explained that the last she had seen of him was when he was on his way down to his uncle's room.

"Are you sure he didn't go into my aunt's room?"

"I really don't know," she said, settling her cap. "It's not my business to put my nose into the guests' affairs."

"Then why do you do it?" I asked simply. But she went off to chase an undergraduate who appeared to be carrying a male urinal, with an air of competent efficiency, into number twenty—which I knew was occupied by a Mrs. Slocum.

I wandered down to my aunt's room and found that she and Edith were both asleep. Edith looked far from comfortable. She had drawn up a straight chair for her feet, and they were considerably higher than her head. The position would have broken a more fragile neck.

Mr. Baker's door was open a little, and I stuck my head in. The old man appeared to be asleep, and Louise had put a towel over the lamp and was sitting there, doing nothing. We exchanged smiles and I withdrew. Louise's resemblance to Frances in that half-light had brought me out in goose-pimples.

I was about to return to the desk, when I noticed a thin thread of light under the door of the room directly opposite my aunt's.

It was the room in which I had looked through the wallet, and I went straight over and pushed the door open.

Trevis was there, searching quietly, as usual.

I went and perched myself on the bed, and it was not until I struck a match for my cigarette that he noticed me. He jumped about a foot in the air and caught his breath sharply.

"My God!" he exclaimed. "You gave me a fright"

"I wouldn't hurt a hair of your head. How did you know that I looked through that wallet in here?"

He grinned at me. "Miss Quinn told me."

"Have you searched my aunt's purse yet?"

He shook his head, and the grin became a bit wry. "She was not partial to the idea."

I laughed, and he gave up searching and leaned against the end of the bed and pulled out his cigarette case. He did not seem to be very happy about it all.

"I'm sure nothing fell out of it while I had it in here," I said after a while.

He said, "No," rather absently.

"What are you looking for?" I asked.

He fixed his eyes on my face for a moment and then dropped them to the tip of his cigarette.

"Oh well," I said cheerfully, "I suppose you won't tell me."

"It really wouldn't interest you."

"I doubt that—but let it go." I told him about Sheila and asked, "What is it that frightens her so?"

He slightly raised his shoulders and said, "Wellaren't you frightened? After what has happened here?"

"Yes," I said frankly, "I am. But Sheila has seen something—more than once. She gives me the creeps when she talks about it—and I guess that is why I'm not in bed, sleeping, right now."

Trevis stirred and disposed of his cigarette. "I've done enough for one night—I'm going to bed. And don't worry about what Sheila says—she's a bit fanciful at times."

We left the room and walked up the hall, and I thought about Sheila being fanciful. Perhaps she was—but certainly there had been someone in the solarium. I had heard the window open and the chair move.

I parted with Trevis at the desk. He said good night politely and disappeared into the guest suite.

Vera was not there, but another nurse approached as I sat down. She hesitated when she saw me, so I said, "Hello," to break the ice.

She came forward slowly. "Are you Miss Warren?"

"Until next Tuesday."

She stared at me, and I felt like an ass. "I'm Jessie Warren," I said.

"Oh. Well—Louise Hoffman said you had my perfume."

CHAPTER TWENTY-SEVEN

I JUMPED UP EAGERLY, and then had to remind myself to be more casual. "If you'll come to my room I'll give it to you."

She said, "All right," and we moved toward the guest suite. When we got inside it was pitch dark, and I began to curse myself for a fool for coming into the place with someone about whom I knew nothing.

My room was in darkness, although I was pretty sure that I had left the light on, and by the time I had groped my way to the switch I had goose-pimples all over me.

I put the light on, and then turned to the nurse—who was stranded in the doorway—and asked her to come in. She closed the door carefully behind her and then asked if she might smoke. I told her to go ahead, and while she was lighting up I took the little bottle from the bureau and gave it to her. "I admire your nerve," I said, perching myself on the arm of a chair. "How could you go into that room and lie down on the bed so soon after someone had been murdered in there?"

She sprang to her feet and gasped, "What do you mean?"

I decided that either her astonishment was genuine or she was doing it very well.

"I mean what I say."

"Somebody murdered?" she stammered. "In that room? "

"Two of them."

"But—"

"Your cigarette is burning a hole in the bedspread," I pointed out. "As for that room—into which you went last night for a nap—both Frances and Olive were murdered there."

She retrieved the cigarette automatically, but her eyes were popping out of her head. "God!" she muttered. "Murdered! It isn't possible."

"It's so just the same. You mean you really didn't know about it?"

"We'd heard there'd been a couple of accidents on the *seventh* floor. But the sixth—and murder—"

Her voice trailed off, and her eyes continued to pop.

"This is the floor all right," I said, "and you were lying on the bed—"

She shivered and said, "Please—how could I know? We never dreamed— Why, it's horrible!"

I said, "Oh well—it's all over. I don't suppose you'll go in there again."

"My God! No! I was a little scared—I thought I was going to get into trouble—but I didn't know it was anything like this. Louise Hoffman just told me that a Miss Warren had found my perfume and for me to go up and get it. I'd never have told anyone that I'd lost it— if I'd known."

"It's all right. Louise won't say anything—and certainly I shan't."

She said, "Thanks. I shouldn't have done it, I guess, but I found my way clear to get a little rest, so I thought I'd sneak up and take it. The perfume must have slipped out of my pocket while I was lying there."

"You went in twice during the evening though, didn't you?" I asked.

"Heavens, no. Only once—quite late—and I straightened up the bed when I left."

"Are you quite sure you didn't go there earlier in the evening?"

"Absolutely certain," she declared vehemently. She was edging toward the door by this time, so I let her go and followed slowly. She peered around the door into the main corridor cautiously and then slipped out and streaked off. I regretted, as I watched her go, that I had not asked her if she had noticed anything peculiar about the room—and then I told myself to stop pretending that I was William Forrest or somebody.

Vera had disappeared, and I sat down in her chair and began to realize that the heat was terrific. The white clock above my head said ten minutes to three, and I wondered idly what I could do with myself—and whether I could possibly go back to my room. But the idea gave me the creeps, and I continued to sit where I was.

Vera came back after a while, her face tight with exasperation.

"What a to-do! Really! That woman—" She told me all about it and how unreasonable most patients were and how, if she ever got sick herself, she would be God's gift to the nursing staff.

I agreed with her thoroughly, and presently she had to go off again. I sighed with relief and got up and walked about a bit, restlessly.

I glanced down the hall and saw that Louise and Edith were there, talking, so I started down to join them. Louise went back into Mr. Baker's room before I got to them, but Edith caught sight of me and waited.

"Why are you walking around at this hour?" she asked as I came up.

"I can't sleep in that rotten guest suite at night," I said gloomily. "I'll have to catch my sleep in the daytime."

"Suit yourself," Edith said, yawning. "Well—I have to do my sleeping now."

"You mean you won't chat with me for a while?"

"No," said Edith, "even if you are the madam's niece."

"I think you're mean. You were talking to Louise."

She yawned again. "That just happened. Mr. Baker keeps her awake a lot of the time, and she happened to catch me when I was awake."

"It's a pity about night nurses," I said, "that they can't get their proper sleep."

"Sarcasm at three in the morning is always wasted on me," said Edith, "and furthermore, you've never been a night nurse."

"What was Louise saying?"

Edith yawned a third time and exposed a fine pair of tonsils. "Frances' funeral is tomorrow—and that poor kid is giving her an expensive one too. That's why she has to keep right on working."

"Maybe we could get Aunt Isabelle to pay for it," I suggested. "And then Louise could go away somewhere for a rest."

"Maybe," said Edith. "But your aunt would have to be approached in the right way—and personally, I can't think of the right way at the present moment."

She went into Aunt Isabelle's room and made quite a racket getting herself settled on the two chairs—but nothing could disturb Aunt Isabelle's sleep when she was properly into it.

I turned away and had a sudden brainwave. I decided to try and sleep in the unoccupied room across the hall.

I went in and stretched out on the bed—but I was instantly wide awake. I got up, searched the room and then closed the door and pushed the bureau in front of it. That relaxed me a bit, and I think I did drowse off for a while, but it was not for long. Something woke me—and although I did not know what it was I felt, somehow, that I had been disturbed in some way.

I could not get back to sleep, and I began to want a cigarette. I had none with me, and I presently remembered that I had left them on the desk. I got up wearily, moved the bureau and went out.

Vera admitted that she had found my cigarettes. She did not, she said, care to have them lying on her desk, so she had taken them to my room. She had supposed, naturally, that I was in my room—and, in fact, where had I been all this time?

I murmured something about my aunt and made for the guest suite. It was after four, but still quite dark, and I groped for my switch in the usual sweat of fear.

The cigarettes were on the bureau, and I snatched them up and started out again. I had left the light on, and when I got to the door I glanced back over my shoulder.

The handle from one of the beds was lying on the floor.

CHAPTER TWENTY-EIGHT

I FAIRLY flew out to the desk and sat down on Vera's chair. My body was shaking and my teeth chattering, and I kept thinking over and over again, "It means another murder—and I must stop it. Somehow I must stop it."

Vera came back, and I told her to phone the police and get William Forrest to come at once. She balked a bit and demanded a lot of explaining before she gave in and lifted the telephone. And then she merely called the office downstairs—and I had only her word for it that they were going to do their part.

I could see that she thought I was being silly and hysterical. "That handle probably fell out," she said. "You've been fooling around with them so much. You'd be better off if you'd mind your own affairs and leave the hospital equipment alone."

"It didn't fall out," I said desperately. "I know that one wasn't loose."

She said, "Tch tch," and went off again.

I sat there for a while, still shivering and calling myself a fool because I could not help feeling glad that I was not a blonde.

I thought of Louise Hoffman and her pretty fair hair, and I couldn't stand it any longer. I went straight down to Mr. Baker's room. I admitted to myself that the whole thing had probably turned my brain a bit—

because why would anyone want to murder only blondes? But I had to make sure that Louise was all right.

I put my head around the door and drew a quick little breath of relief. The old man appeared to be sleeping, and Louise was sitting in the armchair by the shaded light. I made a sound, and when she looked up I beckoned. She came quietly to the door.

"When do you go off duty?" I asked.

"Not until seven. Why?"

"I wish you'd go now," I said unhappily.

"For heaven's sake, why?"

I twisted my handkerchief through my fingers and said stupidly, "You—you're doing too much. You look tired, and you ought to get some sleep. If you'll go now I'll watch Mr. Baker until his morning nurse comes on. It's half-past four now—so it won't be long."

She laughed softly and said, "You're awfully sweet—but I'd have to hand in my thermometer and the buttons of my uniform if I ever did such a thing. You run along to bed and get some sleep."

"Listen," I said desperately, "my aunt is going to give you a present, so that you can go away and take a rest. You won't need this job—and you do need the rest. If you'll only go now you—you can come back at seven, when Miss Cassidy takes over—and nobody need ever know."

She looked at me steadily for a moment and then said firmly, "I'm not going to rat out on my job as long as I can stand on my feet—and I'm not quitting this job either. It suits me—and if it's the last thing I do I intend to find out who is responsible for my sister's death."

I gave it up, then I said miserably, "For God's sake, be careful if you won't go," and walked off.

She must have watched me all the way up the hall, because I turned around when I got to the desk and she was still there. She disappeared when she saw me turn, and I sat down in Vera's empty chair.

I suppose that Louise thought I was completely cracked—and I wasn't sure about it myself. I had no real reason to think that she was intended as the next victim—aside from the fact that she was a blonde—and that sounded more like hysteria than reasoning. As a matter of fact, I could not be at all sure that another victim was intended.

And yet I was desperately uneasy, and I wished intensely that William Forrest would show up.

Vera came back after a while, and I asked her to phone down to the office again, but she said she would do nothing of the kind and, furthermore, I was not to do it either.

The clock said ten to five, and I rumpled my hair fretfully and mutttered, "It ought to be getting light—why is it still so dark?"

"There's a storm coming," Vera said, glancing at the window. "Those clouds are as black as ink. Well—maybe it will cool things off a bit."

She plodded briskly down the corridor, and I was left alone again. I was very tired and very frightened, and I kept thinking, in a confused way, that somebody was going to be murdered before the storm broke and I could not stop it.

Louise appeared after a while, walking toward me up the hall, and I got up to meet her, feeling absurdly relieved at her obvious vitality.

She gave me a brief nod, went past me and made straight for the guest suite!

I ran after her and caught at her arm. "Louise, you can't go in there!"

"Why not?" she said and pulled herself free.

"Oh, don't," I begged, blinking back a sudden film of tears. "Don't go there yet. Wait until it's light—until morning."

Her forehead wrinkled in a little frown of annoyance, and she started on again without a word.

"Wait, please!" I cried. "I'll—tell you something."

I explained about the handle, and she looked at me queerly. "Hasn't it occurred to you," she said, "that if there is something wrong in there the three people who are sleeping there should be warned?"

It had not occurred to me, for the simple reason that I had had a vague, confused idea that the Bakers were responsible for the whole thing anyway.

"Well—but there are two men in there with Sheila," I stammered, "and they ought to be able to look after themselves and her."

Louise wasn't listening. Her eyes were fixed over my shoulder and down the corridor. I swung around, but the corridor stretched empty behind me.

Louise said, "Listen—I have a little errand in the guest suite. You go on back and sit down—I won't be long."

"No," I said hysterically, "I won't. I'm going with you."

"Oh, for heaven's sake, no. It isn't necessary. Look here—if you're worried about that handle—I put it there myself."

She turned away and hurried through the door of the guest suite—
and I was left standing there.

I walked slowly back to the desk and looked at the clock. Half-past
five.

The storm broke then—wild and violent and noisy—but I hardly
noticed it. I kept thinking of Louise and wondering what possible reason she could have for taking that handle out and putting it onto the
floor. I had felt sure that the handle and the murderer were intimately
connected—but I could not picture Louise murdering anyone. And even
supposing she had done it—then why would she admit to having moved
the handle?

I sat there, shivering in the sticky heat and vaguely conscious of
the vivid display of lightning and the crash of thunder.

Vera was still absent, and after a while I realized that Louise had
not come back either. I sat with my eyes glued to the door of the guest
suite, but it remained closed.

I looked at the clock again after what seemed hours. Ten to six.

And then the door to the guest suite opened slowly. I held my breath
and waited—but it was not Louise who came out—it was Sheila Baker.

She wore a negligee which she clutched around her, and her hair
was untidy and her face blotchy. She came straight up to me and stood
in front of me.

"I am not drunk this time," she said steadily, "but I simply cannot
stay in that place any longer. There is something horrible going on in
there."

CHAPTER TWENTY-NINE

"WHAT DO YOU MEAN?" I gasped. "What is it?" She sat down and helped
herself to one of my cigarettes, and I could see that her hands were
shaking badly.

"I don't know—I keep hearing things. I could have sworn I heard a
girl crying in between the thunder a while ago. And then someone
opened a window. But those are only the latest—I've been hearing
noises all night—ever since I saw that horrid thing in the solarium."

"Maybe the window was being closed. I know one of the nurses is in there—and it's pouring rain."

She shook her head. "When those windows are closed you can hear the bump when it comes down. It was being opened." She slumped back in her chair and closed her eyes for a moment. "I could die when I think of how I lay on that horrible bed—the night I was drunk."

I stared at her, while it dawned on me that it must have been Sheila— the first time I had heard someone in my old room—and she had left before we searched it. "You ought to go back to bed," I said, watching her pallid face. "You haven't been well."

"I won't go. Gregg's sleeping like a pig—and if I woke him he'd be disagreeable again about my sleeping in Trevis' bed the other night. Besides, he won't have the light on—he has a perfect mania for going around and switching off lights. And I can't stand the queer noises."

"What was it that frightened you so?" I asked curiously. "In the solarium, I mean—when you fainted?"

She gave her head a little shake and frowned down at her cigarette. "I don't know whether I'm batty—but it's someone I've seen skulking around in there—and I never see the face. If I could just see a white blur that might indicate a face—but it's never there. Only a body—sort of squashy—" She stared into space, her face gray and her eyes dark with horror.

I got up and moved about restlessly. I felt that I should go and look for Louise, but I was afraid. Vera was nowhere to be seen, and I knew Sheila would not come with me.

I pulled the remnants of my courage about me and, facing the guest-suite door, I took a deep breath and plunged through.

It was not so bad after all—it was getting light, and I could see things. I glanced into my room and noticed that the light had been switched off—and the handle was back in its place in the bed. I supposed it was Louise's handiwork and went straight on to the solarium.

Louise was there. She lay on the chaise longue—her head thrown back and her eyes closed. There was no one else about, and she appeared to be sleeping peacefully.

I admired her beauty for a moment and then backed out quietly. I decided to let her sleep until just before seven o'clock, when I would wake her in time for her to get back to Mr. Baker's room before Miss Cassidy came on.

I went back to the desk and found Sheila still sitting there. "It's morning," I said. "We could both go to bed and to sleep now."

"We could go to bed," she said bitterly. "God knows whether I'll ever be able to sleep again after all this horror. But I'm not going back in there."

It was still too early to wake Louise, so I wandered down the hall to my aunt's room.

To my surprise I found her wide awake, and she hailed me imperiously. "I'm glad to see you up so early in the morning, Jessie. You seem to be getting into better habits. Give Edith a poke, will you? I want her to wash my face."

I gave Edith a poke, and she came to with a subdued yell.

"Shame to disturb you," said my aunt acidly. "But you can't sleep there all day."

Edith yawned and straightened her cap. "Did you want anything?"

"Not a thing," said Aunt Isabelle furiously. "I'd just as leave lie dirty here."

Edith yawned again, mechanically prepared a basin of warm water and then brought a cup to the bed. Aunt Isabelle slipped her upper and lower plates into it. "Take them outthide and clean them," she lisped. "I want to talk to Jethie anyway."

Edith departed, and my aunt turned to me with a satisfied air. "Now, Jethie, your worrieth are over. I got Michael to agree to marry you."

I said, "Oh, good! I've been worried sick. As for these murders—"

"Be quiet!" she snapped. "I fully understhand the theriouthness of what hath happened here. But all thith will be unimportant in a few weekth—and you thtill have your future before you."

"All right—go ahead," I said resignedly.

"If you marry Michael I shall thettle fifty thouthand dollarth on you!" she announced triumphantly.

I staggered, and my jaw dropped nearly to my chest. Fifty thousand to Michael—and the same to me! I wondered, dizzily, if she were right in the head.

"I knew you'd be thtunned," she said, looking pleased. "But I want you properly thettled."

In the midst of a volume of profuse thanks that I poured over her Edith returned with her plates, and I made my escape.

No girl, I thought hysterically, could be expected to turn down both Michael and fifty thousand dollars—even if it meant living with guinea pigs.

I raced to the telephone and called my home. Lenore answered after a while, her voice full of sleep. I told her she was to bring over some hats as soon as she was dressed.

"Are you out of your mind?" she demanded, outraged. "Waking me in the small hours of the morning to ask for hats. You can't wear hats around a hospital."

"It's nearly seven o'clock," I said, "and I want those hats. Don't fail me."

"You're cracked—you must be. And Mother says you're to come home anyway."

"I'm not coming home. If I stay here there's a chance I'll land both Michael and fifty thousand dollars."

I heard her give an excited squeal, but I slammed down the receiver and hurried to the guest suite. It was a few minutes before seven, and I wanted to get Louise back to her patient before she got into trouble.

Trevis was in my room. I supposed, indifferently, that he was searching as usual, and I paused at the door and said, "Go right ahead—don't apologize."

He laughed uncomfortably. "Please don't be angry—but the piece of paper we're looking for means a great deal to us, and I thought perhaps you might have mislaid it in here."

"I thought you'd looked here already."

He dropped rather heavily onto the bed and passed his hand across his forehead, "I suppose I did. I've done nothing but search for days, and I'm sick of it. The thing must be somewhere—but I'm damned if I can find it."

"Why don't you tell what it is? I might be able to help you."

But he shook his head and said rather formally, "I'm sorry to keep barging into your room all the time. You've been very good-natured about it."

I said it was all right and went on to the solarium. Windows were open at each end, and there was a strong draft blowing through. Louise was still lying on the chaise longue, and her blonde hair was blowing about her face. I took a step toward her and then stopped. There was something about her. I felt my hands clenching, and my breath came faster.

I saw the pot just before it fell. It was a rubber plant in a china bowl, and it rested on a tall iron stand. The plant was too heavy for the bowl, and the wind caught at the leaves and tipped it. I strangled a scream as it fell and saw it land squarely on Louise's hand. It shattered, and pieces of dirt and china scattered over the floor.

But Louise didn't mind at all. She did not move—and as far as I could see her hand wasn't even bleeding.

CHAPTER THIRTY

I KNEW what it meant, of course. If I looked at the back of her head I would find blood. And the sun was pouring in at the windows.

I began to scream—shrilly, and without much expression. Nobody came to help me, and Louise lay there, with her eyes closed and the blonde hair blowing about her forehead.

I woke up in bed, with Michael's face suspended eerily above me.

I blinked at it and said, "Look at the handle—it must be covered with blood."

"It's all right," Michael said soothingly. "We're not in the guest suite. This room is right across the hall from your aunt's."

I raised my head, and a slow glance around showed me that this was true. I relaxed against the pillow and stared up at Michael. "You know I'm never going back there again," I said earnestly.

"No, of course not. But I want you to sleep now."

Miss Zimmerman materialized at my side with some sort of pill or capsule rattling around in a paper cup and a glass of water in her other hand for washing it down.

I swallowed the thing indifferently and raised my eyes to Michael's face, "She's dead, isn't she?"

He nodded. "Don't concentrate on it. Take a look at the hats Lenore brought you this morning. What's the matter with her, anyway?"

"I don't know," I said dully. "I guess she's crazy, like Aunt Isabelle."

Michael left then, and I went to sleep..

It was almost dark when I woke up, and Miss Gould was standing at the bureau. She was trying on my hats. Lenore had brought three, and Miss Gould had just placed my newest and best on her head. It gave me a certain amount of pleasure to note that it did not suit her.

"Try one of the others," I suggested, "and turn on the light so that I can see better."

She shied like a startled horse and pulled the hat off. "Oh, I beg your pardon," she murmured.

"Try the others," I insisted. "Anything to forget this dreadful place."

She said soberly, "It is dreadful. I just hate to come here any more."

"Try the hats on."

She tried them on happily, but they did not look well on her, and I began to get worried about them. It wasn't reasonable that they should look like New Year's Eve on her and yet be as stunning on me as I had supposed.

William Forrest came in after a tentative little knock, and I forgot about the hats and was dragged back again into all the horror. I wished, miserably, that I had nothing more than a few hats on my mind.

"I should like to speak to Miss Warren alone," Forrest said, eying first Miss Gould and then the hats.

Miss Gould glanced doubtfully at me. "Did Doctor Rand say—"

"Doctor Rand said I was not to wake her—but he gave permission to question her as soon as she did wake."

Miss Gould frowned her disapproval and walked out of the room with one of my hats still on her head.

I could not concentrate on Forrest after she had gone, because I was listening for Aunt Isabelle's reaction to the sight of Miss Gould wearing my hat.

I had not long to wait. There was a vocal explosion, and Miss Gould came flying across the hall and tore the hat from her head. She was in tears.

I interrupted Forrest—I hadn't been listening to him anyway—and told Miss Gould not to be a fool. "How do you expect to get anywhere as a nurse when you let your crank patients upset you? Don't pay any attention to her."

Miss Gould, dabbing at her eyes, urged me to be a nurse sometime and see how I liked it.

I told her I had a job all lined up as a street cleaner and thought I'd try that first.

William Forrest cleared his throat and said mildly, "May I have your attention?"

Miss Gould departed, and I told him all about it. He asked innumerable questions, which I answered as well as I could, and after about an hour of it he left me, after thanking me politely.

I looked at my watch and found that it was nine o'clock. I stretched, yawned and then got out of bed and went across to my aunt's room.

"Miss Gould," I said, "I'm starving. Do you think—"

"Go and get her something to eat," said Aunt Isabelle. "Jessie, come here and make yourself comfortable in the armchair. I hope you're feeling better—although why you must needs throw a fit just because you see a bit of life in the raw I can't think."

"How are you feeling?" I asked, and when she was well launched I sat back and attended to my own thoughts.

William Forrest had told me nothing—he had simply asked questions and listened. I wondered what had really happened to Louise— and whether the handle in my old room was bloodstained. I wondered, too, why Forrest had not come when I sent for him. I had told him about my effort to get him, when I found the handle lying on the floor— and although he had seemed very interested he had volunteered no explanation.

I broke into Aunt Isabelle's symptoms and asked about Louise.

"Dead," she said, her eyes snapping with excitement. "Killed in the same way. And that handle in your bedroom covered with blood."

"How do you know?" I asked, feeling as though I were going to be sick.

"I sent Miss Zimmerman to find out."

I rested my head against the back of my chair and wondered drearily if I could somehow have saved Louise. But I could not stop her bodily from going into the guest suite—and then she had put me off by saying that she had dropped that handle onto the floor herself. She must have been lying, of course, in order to get rid of me—which meant that she was very anxious to get in there alone. And she had gone straight in to her death.

Miss Gould came back with my tray and fussed around a bit, hoping I would like it because it was all she could find.

The meal consisted of jelly, junket, broth, toast and coffee. I sighed. "It's all right," I said politely. "All I wanted was steak and French-fried potatoes—but this will do very well."

Miss Gould said, "I'm sorry," rather helplessly, and Aunt Isabelle snapped, "Be quiet—both of you!"

"Now, Jessie, what under the shining sun possessed you to make Lenore bring those hats around? The Forrest man was decidedly suspicious. He said it wasn't normal for a girl to order a collection of hats when she's staying in a hospital and has no intention of going out. He indicated to me that perhaps you were a little feeble-minded."

"What did you say?"

"I told him I hadn't noticed it particularly."

I said, "Thanks."

"And then he asked if you had ever shown any signs of violence, and of course I had to tell him that you had. Remember that time you slapped Lenore's face and pulled her hair—and the other time when you kicked that beau of yours? Now, what was his name?"

I got up and left the room. "At least," I said over my shoulder, "a padded cell will be quiet and peaceful."

I met Edith just outside, and her eyes were popping. "My God! What happened here this morning? The girls are all talking downstairs. I swear I'm not going to stay here—I'm scared stiff."

Aunt Isabelle called her at that point, and she went into the room.

I took a walk up the hall. I did not want to go back to bed, and I was battling a strong desire to pack my things and go straight home.

Halfway to the desk I noticed a piece of paper lying on the floor, and I stooped idly and picked it up. It was folded, and I opened it out and looked at it.

I stopped dead and stared at the thing. It was the last will and testament of Ames Baker, written in red ink, and it was brief and to the point. It left everything of which he died possessed to Olive Parsons.

CHAPTER THIRTY-ONE

I MUST HAVE READ that will through at least a dozen times. It was a short, legal-sounding document—and it had been witnessed by Agnes Gaffney and Frances Hoffman!

I refolded it and went along to the desk, clutching it firmly in my hand.

Vera looked up and said curtly, "You're supposed to stay in bed."

"All right—but I want you to get William Forrest for me—I must see him."

She said, "You're to go back to bed at once. And as for that Forrest, I've seen too much of him as it is. I don't care if he never comes back."

"Very well—don't get him," I said furiously. "Maybe Louise would be alive right now if you'd got him here last night when I asked you to."

She gave an outraged little shriek. "What are you talking about? I phoned the office last night—you heard me yourself—but I suppose they thought we were being hysterical up here and didn't bother."

I shrugged and she added angrily, "That's the second time I've been accused of letting that poor girl die."

She was right, of course. She had phoned the office—and if the message had never been put through the fault was down there.

"I absolutely refuse to be involved again," Vera went on. "You go on into the guest suite. There's a man there looking after things—Forrest left him, and he's supposed to stay there. If you want anything you can tell him about it."

I felt that it was urgent about the will, so I took a long breath and went through the door into the guest suite.

The hall light was still out, but the solarium was brilliantly lighted, and I could hear the Bakers talking together in there. Light came from my room, too, and I went to the door and looked in.

A man was stretched comfortably on the bed, reading a newspaper, with a cigar in his mouth and his shoes dirtying up the counterpane. He pulled the cigar out of his mouth when he saw me and raised a pair of black brows inquiringly.

I asked him to get hold of William Forrest, as I had something important to show him.

"Won't I do, lady?"

"No," I said, "I want Mr. Forrest."

"O.K.," he said, returning the cigar to his mouth and picking up the newspaper again. "Only you'll have to wait till tomorrow. He's gone to a dance."

"Gone to a dance!" I gasped in utter amazement.

"That's what I said, lady."

"But—with all this going on?" It seemed incredible somehow.

"Yeah," said the voice from behind the newspaper. "Those guys gotta have time off like anyone else."

I flounced out of the room and went back to the desk in the main corridor. I was somehow shocked to think that William Forrest would be so little concerned as to go to a dance.

Vera was busy writing, and Edith had come up and was sitting in a chair and yawning her head off. They were ostentatiously ignoring each other.

As I approached Edith stood up and contrived to jog Vera's elbow. The fountain pen went wild for an instant, and Vera sprang to her feet, her eyes blazing with fury.

The impending battle was averted when Dr. Hammond stepped out of the elevator. Vera straightened her cap and produced a smile, and Edith turned to me with a businesslike air which suggested that she had a message to deliver before she hurried back to her patient.

I knew Dr. Hammond. He had attended my aunt until he suggested that she try walking more and eating less.

He smiled at me and said, "Back again? How's Miss Daniel?"

"You go and ask her," I said. "I never can remember offhand."

He laughed, and he and Vera went off down the hall.

"Where are the Bakers?" Edith asked abruptly.

"In the guest suite."

"Then go and get one of them to stay with the old man, will you? I'm doing what I can, but he shouldn't be alone, and they're having a devil of a time getting someone to take the case."

"Poor old soul," I said, shaking my head. "It's a shame."

"Don't worry about him," Edith said shortly. "He's all right."

"But I thought he was dying?"

She made a grimace. "I doubt it."

"Well, anyway," I said firmly, "the Bakers are in the solarium, and you can go and get them if you want to. I won't go in there again for anybody."

"Oh, all right. I can only get killed."

"Aren't Vera and her stooges supposed to take care of him when he has no nurse of his own?" I asked.

"Sure—but the old boy is used to refined treatment. He wouldn't want a butcher like Vera doing things for him."

She departed for the guest suite, and I went slowly down the hall toward my aunt's room. I could hear her snores before I got there, so I detoured into Mr. Baker's room.

He was lying quietly, with his eyes closed. I looked at him for a while, but I could not tell whether he was very ill or not. Nor did I know whether he was sleeping, unconscious or just resting. At any rate, he made no movement, and I allowed my eyes to wander around the room.

Suddenly from the door a sharp voice asked, "What do you want?" I turned quickly and met Gregg's cold, suspicious eyes.

"I beg your pardon," I said frigidly. "I was watching your uncle until Edith could get one of you to do it."

"Thank you." His tone was ungracious, and I saw his gaze fasten on the will that was still folded tightly in my hand.

He took a step forward, and his attitude was faintly menacing. "What have you got there?"

But I had had time to think. I glanced at the will carelessly. "It's a list of errands that my aunt wants me to see to tomorrow. If you're really interested I'll read them off to you."

"I'm sorry," he said and didn't look it. "I thought it might be something you had picked up in here."

I walked out of the room and spared a moment of pity for Sheila. No wonder she prefers Trevis, I thought, to that bad-tempered lump.

My aunt was still snoring, and Edith was settling herself into the armchair with a fan and a glass of ice water within stretching distance.

I left them to it and went across the hall to my room. I put the will carefully under my pillow and then washed up a bit and got into bed.

I had slept all day and was wide-awake, so I lit a cigarette and then regretted that I had not a book or some magazines—but I could not force myself to get up and find some.

I began to get nervous after a while. Aunt Isabelle and Edith were sleeping comfortably—Gregg was watching his uncle—and I was lying all alone with a piece of dynamite under my pillow.

I was just about to get up when I heard quiet footsteps crossing the hall to my door. I waited, with my heart in my mouth, and then the door opened noiselessly and Edith looked in.

She said, "Oh—you're awake. I can't sleep—I'm too nervous."

"Come on in," I said, feeling weak with relief. "I can't sleep either."

We talked for a while, and I asked her about Olive Parsons. "Had she been with the Bakers for very long?"

"About two years, I think," Edith said. "He's had a nurse for at least five years."

"Do you know who he had before Olive then?"

She said, "Sure. Frances Hoffman."

CHAPTER THIRTY-TWO

"FRANCES HOFFMAN!" I said stupidly. "But why didn't you tell me?"

"Why should I?" said Edith. "You never asked me."

"Well, but—but you knew I'd be interested. You might have told me."

She shrugged. "I never thought of it."

"Why didn't she keep on with private nursing then? Instead of doing floor work here?"

"Don't ask me," said Edith. "I wouldn't know."

"It's tied up together someway," I said. "Frances and Olive both worked for Mr. Baker—and they both get killed. And then Louise too."

"In that case," said Edith, "it's my turn next, or Vera's. We've both worked for him."

I said, "For heaven's sake, what is this? Has he had all the nurses working for him at one time or another?"

"Darn near," Edith said. "There were several before me, and I lasted a year. Then Vera—she hung on for seven months. She set her cap for him, but it didn't work and she finally left. Seven months in any one place was a record for her anyway—and that's the reason she's doing floor work now—because in private practice she couldn't get on with anyone. After Vera left there were several, one after another, and then came Frances, who was there for two months. Then Olive took him over. She was able to manage him better than anyone."

"Do you mean he's hard to get on with?" I asked. "He seems quite mild."

Edith gave a short laugh. "He's the most unreasonable, bad-tempered old bastard I've ever known. That's why I can take your aunt—

I came straight to her from him—and her disposition seemed quite sunny after his."

I thought it over for a while and then said, "Edith, what's the connection? There must be something."

"What do you mean?"

"Well, why were Frances and Olive both killed?"

"You forgot Louise," Edith said dryly.

"But I feel sure that if Louise had not come here she wouldn't have been murdered."

"Why?"

"I don't know exactly," I said slowly. "Except, perhaps, that she told me she was going to get to the bottom of Frances' death."

"Sounds like dangerous business," Edith admitted.

"It's possible," I went on thoughtfully, "that Louise knew something about it—Frances might have told her something at one time or another."

"Maybe."

"At first," I said, "I thought Frances was murdered because she was mistaken for Olive—it was easy to confuse them from the back view. But since Frances worked for Mr. Baker, and Olive, too—I guess the three of them were intended to die—Louise, because she knew something about it."

"Why did you think Olive was supposed to be murdered and not Frances?" Edith asked.

I nearly told her about the will but stopped on the verge of it. I knew she was a gossip, and I was afraid she might tell someone. I said instead, "Because Olive was killed second—so *she* couldn't have been mistaken for Frances."

"Maybe you're trying to make reason where there isn't any," Edith said after a while. "It might be a maniac who just doesn't care for blondes."

I shuddered and lay for a while, staring at the ceiling.

"Did Louise ever work for Mr. Baker before?" I asked presently.

"I don't think so—I never heard of it anyway."

"Is he a ladies' man?"

Edith hesitated. "I don't know exactly. He could give you hell one minute—and then turn around and send you flowers."

"Did the three Bakers live with him when you were his nurse?"

"No," said Edith. "They visited him occasionally—but not often."

"Mistake," I murmured absently.

"Why?"

"Oh well—you should visit a rich uncle fairly frequently."

"They came as often as he let them," Edith said grimly.

"Has he been an invalid all this time?"

"More or less. His heart's bad—but he got around plenty."

"Who did he go around with?"

"The nurses mostly," Edith said, laughing a little. "Present or ex. He asked me out to dinner several times after I had left."

I glanced at her in some surprise. It seemed odd that he should part with his nurses in anger—and then invite them out to dinner. "Did you go?"

"Sure. Catch me turning down a free meal?"

"Seems funny," I said reflectively, "a rich man like that—going out only with his nurses. Weren't there other women that he could have gone around with?"

"Plenty—he was always getting invitations—but he turned them down. Said he preferred the nurses."

I was quiet for a while, thinking it over. The old man had left everything to Olive—so he must have been in love with her. And probably the other Bakers had known something of it. They must have known about the will—hence the frantic search. Olive, the beneficiary, and Frances, one of the witnesses, had both been murdered—and then Louise, who was very likely in Frances' confidence. It looked bad for the younger Bakers—and yet somebody else had been playing hide-and-seek with the will. Who? And why?

"What are you thinking about?" Edith asked.

"Just thinking it over."

"Young girl solves hospital murders and embarrasses police," she said derisively.

"You can laugh—but I know something that the police don't."

"What's that?"

"I must ask you to be quiet," Vera's voice said suddenly from the door. "There are sick people trying to sleep. Miss Quinn, your patient wants you."

"O.K.," said Edith and got to her feet. She went on out, and Vera advanced to my bedside.

"I should try and sleep, if I were you."

"Thanks for the advice," I said shortly.

She went out, and I settled down to try and sleep, after first making sure that the will was still under my pillow.

It was no use though. I was wide awake, and I could not stop thinking about the whole thing. It seemed to me that it must be the Bakers—one or all of them—and I fastened on Gregg as the leader. I felt that if I could only creep up on one of their confabs I might hear something of value.

I could not lie there any longer after a while, so I got up, put on a negligee and pinned the will to the inside of my nightgown. I went along to the chartroom and found Vera at the desk.

I asked her straight out about her sojourn with Mr. Baker, and she had plenty to say about it. According to her, Ames Baker was a nasty old man, who showered unwelcome attentions on her until she had to leave in self-defense. Nothing, she said, would ever induce her to attend him again.

I asked her if she was quite sure that she had not accepted any of his attentions, and she got quite huffy about it. She gave me to understand that she had given him the frigid treatment from first to last.

I asked if he had ever invited her out after she had left him. She actually blushed and said yes, she had gone out with him once, but she had been so cold that he had not asked her again.

She had to go then, and I sat there, looking at the door that led into the guest suite. I kept thinking that the Bakers might be having one of their serious discussions and, since they knew I was not sleeping there, it might be loud enough to catch an ear—if that ear were laid against their door. I couldn't resist it after a while. I made up my mind just to slip in and then, if everything was quiet, I could slip out again.

The hall was in total darkness, as usual, when I got inside, and I crept quietly to Trevis' door. There was no sound from inside, so I went on to the Gregg Bakers' room. All was quiet there, too, and I turned away—and froze into my tracks.

Between me and the door into the main corridor was Sheila's Thing.

CHAPTER THIRTY-THREE

IT WAS TOO DARK to see very much, but I could make out the irregular, lightish outline of a body—and certainly there was no indication of a head or face.

I couldn't scream—my throat seemed to be paralyzed. I backed to the door behind me, pushed it open and stumbled into the Gregg Bakers' room. There was no light, and I closed the door with flat, sweating palms and leaned against it—my heart thudding in my ears.

I remained there for a few minutes of absolute silence, and then my voice came back and I whispered urgently, "Oh, please help me."

There was no reply and no sound, and I turned my head fearfully and looked about the room. It was pretty dark, but a faint glow from the windows brought the beds into relief—and they were empty. I was alone then—with that squashy, headless body in the hall and no lock on the door. For a period of wild indecision I just stood there—pressing my weight against the door—and then I remembered the bureau.

I stumbled madly through the dark, caught at the clumsy piece of furniture and swung it round against the door.

My terror eased off a bit, and I found my way to the switch and turned the light on. The room was empty, but I looked nervously into the bathroom and under both beds.

I sat down and wondered what to do next. I considered screaming but decided against it, as being too embarrassing. After all, what *had* I seen? I couldn't describe it very well, and I knew I'd be accused of hysteria.

In the end I made up my mind to leave the bedroom door wide open, so that the light would shine into the hall, and simply make a dash for it. In the meantime, while I was trying to stiffen my courage, I made an automatic and desultory search of the room.

There was nothing much but clothes and Sheila's cosmetics until I came to the wastebasket. There was one crumpled piece of paper there, and I smoothed it out carefully. It was a note, signed "Sheila" and presumably addressed to Gregg.

"That black devil insulted me again today. Am not staying here any longer."

I studied it for a while, but I could not make anything of it, so I pinned it into my nightgown, along with the will.

I had my hands on the bureau, preparatory to moving it, when I heard a sound in the hall. I listened fearfully, but the footsteps were firm and unselfconscious, and the next instant I heard my name called and knew that it was Michael.

I pushed the bureau away from the door and flew out to him, with a gasp of relief.

He was decidedly cross. He said, "When I leave instructions for you to stay in bed I expect you to stay there. I've been looking all over the place for you—but I never dreamed that you'd be stupid enough to come in here."

"Please!" I said. "I have a headache."

"You're damned lucky," he said coldly, "to have enough of your head left to ache."

He caught my arm and marched me out of the door and all the way down the corridor to my new room. He helped me into the high narrow bed and pulled the covers up to my chin.

When I had recovered my breath I said, "Have you ever tried that sort of treatment on Aunt Isabelle? I think it would do her more good than a week at the seashore."

He ignored me and settled himself into the armchair. I thought he looked tired and worried, and I wondered, with a flash of jealousy, if he were mourning Louise. I wanted to ask him and then felt ashamed of the impulse and decided, unhappily, to let him grieve in peace.

I realized suddenly that the bedclothes were still up around my chin, where Michael had tucked them, and I was practically smothering in the heat. I kicked them off, lit a cigarette and wondered why he was sitting there.

He glanced at me and said absently, "I think I'll cut you down to twelve cigarettes a day."

"How do you aim to do that?" I asked with genuine interest.

Before he could reply Vera pushed into the room with a tray of coffee. She gave me a very frosty look and produced a nice smile for Michael, which was wasted because he wasn't looking. He cast a vague eye at the tray and asked her to put it on the table beside my bed.

She lowered it, with a bit of a clatter, and said defensively, "I can't help it if Miss Warren will go running all over the hospital."

Michael said, "Beat it."

She went, and after a moment I said soberly, "I'm very sorry, Michael—about Louise, I mean."

He came out of his abstraction rather abruptly and really looked at me. "What are you getting at? Of course you're sorry—so am I. A young girl like that—three of them. I don't know what the hell the police think they're doing."

"There's a man staying in the guest suite tonight," I said. "And by the way, if you're not too wrapped up in your thoughts, will you kindly wind this bed up to a sitting position? I can't drink coffee lying flat on my back—and I'm afraid to get out of bed while you're looking."

He got up and banged around with one of the handles until he had me practically leaning forward. "There's a man there, right enough," he said. "Sleeping peacefully on your bed."

I wondered if it could have been the cop that I had seen in the hall —but I thought not. I knew he was wearing a dark suit and the shape I had seen was lightish.

Michael poured the coffee and handed me a cup. "What were you doing up there when I yanked you out?"

I told him all about it, and as I had expected he was unimpressed. "You didn't see anything, Jessie—your nerves are all shot to hell. I'm going to keep you in this bed if I have to chain you down."

I did not tell him about the will or Sheila's note, because I knew he'd take them away from me, and I wanted to hand them over to Forrest myself.

I didn't care so much about the note, but it was pinned in with the will, and if Michael thought I was withholding anything he had only to arm himself with a stethoscope, as an excuse, and search until he found it. As it was, I had a nervous idea that every time I breathed I crackled slightly.

"How's Mr. Baker?" I asked politely.

He put his cup down and opened his cigarette case. "What's your interest? Does Trevis inherit? And even if he does—you'll kindly remember that you're mine. I saw you first."

"Me and fifty thousand dollars," I said bitterly.

"Right."

"Don't you ever sleep?" I asked crossly. "You seem to be here at all hours of the day and night. Do you expect me to spend my married life in a little trundle bed of my own—and taking a guinea pig's temperature by way of amusement?"

He said, "Don't be indecent, Jessie. Also, if you can take a guinea pig's temperature, alone and unaided, I'll personally undertake to eat my hat. When I get you—and that formidable aunt of yours—out of here I'm going to catch up on a lot of sleep."

"You mean you're watching over us?" I asked, touched.

"You—plus fifty thousand dollars and a steady income—yes."

He wound the bed down again and then came around and kissed me. "Good night, darling. I love you, even if you are dumb and have red hair and a fearful aunt."

He went off, and I lay there with my head in a whirl. I told myself six or seven times that of course he hadn't meant it—but I couldn't get myself to believe it. I gave up at last and thought fiercely, "All right— go ahead and enjoy it until your fool's paradise comes crashing down about your ears."

It was a long time before I slept, because I couldn't get Michael out of my mind—but I must have dozed off eventually. I know I woke up suddenly with a sharp sense of having been disturbed.

I moved my arm—and my hand touched another hand. Another hand that was not mine.

CHAPTER THIRTY-FOUR

THE HAND was withdrawn instantly, and someone went quickly and quietly out of the room. I fumbled desperately with the light and got it on at last—and looked fearfully around the room. I was alone as far as I could see, and I got out of bed and ran to the door. I wrenched it open and looked up the hall—but it stretched away from me, dimly lighted and empty.

I thought of the will then. I had unpinned it from my nightgown and had placed it, together with the note, under my pillow. I went back into the room and pulled the pillow from the bed—and discovered that they were both gone.

I was suddenly more angry than frightened. I slipped into the white chiffon negligee and went across the hall to my aunt's room. Aunt Isabelle was snoring loudly, and Edith was sleeping peacefully in the chair. I shook Edith gently by the shoulder, and she came to with a start.

"What's the matter?" she whispered irritably. "Why can't you go to bed and stay there?"

"Come out into the hall for a minute," I whispered back.

She adjusted her cap and followed me unwillingly, and when I had got her outside I asked if she had seen or heard anyone sneaking around.

"No," she said flatly. "And if I did I wouldn't care."

"Somebody came into my room."

"So what?" said Edith.

Her mood was distinctly noncooperative, so I let her go and I slipped into Mr. Baker's room. He was alone and lying quietly with his eyes closed. I glanced around briefly and then went out again, wondering whether Edith was still looking after him or whether Vera had taken over.

I went along to the chartroom and found Vera at the desk. The sight of me annoyed her, and she made no effort to conceal it. "Why can't you stay in bed?" she said angrily. "Doctor Rand blames me for letting you get up—and what am I to do about it?"

"Nothing," I said shortly. "Tell me, who's been down my end of the hall?"

"Why?"

"Someone's been in my room. Stealing."

"Stealing!" she gasped.

"Yes. Who was down that way?"

"What was stolen?" Vera asked, registering astonishment, annoyance and eager interest all at the same time.

"Something important," I said coldly. "I'm asking you who went down that way."

"But I don't know," she declared impatiently. "I've been busy, on and off, for the last hour. I do know that those three Bakers came up in the elevator about half an hour ago."

"Did they go down to Mr. Baker's room?"

"I couldn't tell you," she said, shaking her head. "I merely saw them come out of the elevator. I have no idea which way they went."

"Did you see them leave earlier on?"

"No—certainly not. I have enough to do without keeping track of the guests' arrivals and departures."

I was silent for a moment and then I asked, "Who is supposed to be caring for Mr. Baker now—you or Edith?"

"I am—of course. That busybody Quinn woman wanted to shoulder her way in—but naturally it was not allowed."

"Are you glad?"

"Glad?" she repeated, elevating her eyebrows.

"I mean are you glad to look after him? Do you like him? "

"You know quite well what I think of him," she said indignantly. "I look after him because it is my duty as a nurse."

"All right," I said, "I apologize. Where's that policeman? The one who's guarding this floor?"

"I have no idea, I'm sure."

"But I must see him," I said. "At once."

"Quite all right with me," said Vera and took up her fountain pen.

I said, "Won't you please come into the guest suite with me while I get him?"

"No."

I looked at the door that led into the guest suite and knew that I simply could not go through it alone.

"Vera," I said desperately, "either you come with me or I'll put in a complaint about you."

The fountain pen faltered, and she raised cold, suspicious little eyes to my face. "What are you talking about? What kind of a complaint?"

"I'll think up several—and I'll make them juicy enough to give you a nice black eye. You won't be able to do a thing but deny them."

"That's unfair!" she cried, flinging down the pen.

"I don't care. It's unfair of you not to come with me while I get that man."

She got up and started toward the guest suite without another word, but her eyes were snapping with fury.

We had a bit of trouble getting the policeman awake, but once he understood what I wanted he came with me amiably enough. We went back to the chartroom, and I told him that he'd have to get hold of Forrest at once.

He looked at his watch and murmured, "Two-thirty. I'll see if I can catch him."

He went off to the phone booth, and Vera asked me why I wanted Forrest in such a hurry. She suggested that perhaps I was in love with him and merely wanted to see him.

I asked her how she'd guessed it and declared that I was crazy about Forrest and would use any excuse to get him near me.

She clicked her tongue, shook her head and said, "Doctor Rand is such a nice man too."

The plainclothes man came back from the telephone booth and said that William Forrest was coming, but how about telling him while I was waiting?

I refused, but he spent the next ten minutes trying to make me change my mind. He went off in a huff at last, presumably back to bed.

Forrest stepped out of the elevator about half an hour later, and I took him out of hearing distance of Vera and told him the whole thing.

He was very much put out about the will and the note having been stolen and said that if I had only given them to the man he had left in charge it would have been much better.

"However," he added grimly, "they are probably somewhere on this floor—and they're going to be found." He went to the door of the guest suite and called, "Bill."

I heard Bill reply and then Forrest went in, and the door closed behind him.

"Bill" reminded me of my Saturday-night date, and I realized, with a little gasp of dismay, that this was Saturday and I had missed the whole affair. I was surprised to find that I did not care very much after all—but I felt rather guilty about Bill. I had not even telephoned to explain that I couldn't go.

Sheila came out of the guest suite, attired in a sheer negligee, and joined us at the desk. She looked at me and said, "Have you a cigarette?"

"No smoking here, please," Vera said crisply.

I supplied Sheila and lighted one myself. "What's the matter?" I asked curiously.

"Matter! What in God's name are they doing in here? They came in and said they were very sorry but they'd have to search our rooms."

"I don't know what they're doing," I said airily.

Vera glanced up from her writing and said reprovingly, "You

shouldn't tell lies."

Sheila narrowed her eyes slightly and stared at me, and I felt myself blushing. "I don't actually know what's going on," I said defensively. "But something was stolen from me tonight, and I told them about it—so maybe that's what they're looking for."

Sheila colored angrily and said, "One of us is supposed to be the thief, I dare say. What is it that was stolen from you?"

"I'm afraid I can't tell you," I said, carefully flicking ash onto the floor. "It's supposed to be a secret."

"Oh," said Sheila coldly. "Sorry."

A short uncomfortable silence was broken by the footsteps of a Negro orderly, dressed in his blue-and-white hospital suit, who shuffled across the main corridor in front of us. He went into the service elevator.

Something about him struck me as familiar, and suddenly I grabbed Sheila's arm. "There goes your 'Thing,' " I cried.

CHAPTER THIRTY-FIVE

SHEILA got slowly to her feet and stared. The man was still in the elevator, fussing around with some pails, and we both looked at him for nearly a minute of silence.

"Why, I—you're right," Sheila whispered finally. "It is—it's that thing. He must have been in there." She gave a sudden shrill giggle. "Squashy body and no face. His face was so black I couldn't see it." She sat down again, still shaken with hysterical laughter.

Vera gave her a professional glance and said, "Now, now—what's this all about?"

I gestured toward the orderly and asked, "What business has he in the guest suite?"

"None whatever," Vera said in some surprise. "But he's not in the guest suite—and furthermore, he never goes there."

"You have your neck out, Daisy," I said coldly. "He does go there—and often."

Vera's bosom swelled, and her eyes began to snap. "I beg your pardon," she said formally, "but that orderly never sets foot in the guest suite at any time."

"Never mind about my pardon. I'm telling you that he does."

The bone of contention shut the elevator door at that point and disappeared from view.

"I wish you'd go to bed," Vera said crossly.

"We must get hold of him," said Sheila nervously, "and ask him what he was doing in there."

"We could tell the police and let them question him," I suggested.

But Sheila said, "No," before the words were well out of my mouth. "Let's talk to him first—we can tell the police later."

"He never went into the guest suite," said Vera monotonously.

"Oh, change the record," I said and went down the hall before she could blow up. I could hear her telling Sheila all about it instead.

I headed for my aunt's room, but when I came to Mr. Baker's door I heard him talking, so I went in and listened.

He was moving his head and picking restlessly at the bedclothes with his hands, and he repeated over and over again, "It will be all right when I find it."

I felt that somebody had been remiss in not having eased his mind, so I decided to do it myself. I leaned over and said quietly, "It's all right, Mr. Baker. We found it and put it away for you."

He opened his eyes suddenly and looked straight into my face. "Found it?" he said quite rationally. "Good! Where did you put it?"

I was surprised at his coherence, and for a moment I hesitated. I felt pretty sure, somehow, that he did not want his relatives to know anything about it. Finally I told him that it was in his bureau drawer.

"Oh, that's good," he said, closing his eyes again. "Good—very good. I might die, you know—and I wanted things to be right for the right person." He gave a queer little laugh. "It would be funny if she found out."

"Who?" I asked eagerly.

But he seemed to have forgotten me. "I'm glad I didn't die sooner," he muttered. "My affairs are in good shape now."

"That's nice," I said inanely. And then, on a sudden inspiration, I asked, "What did Agnes Gaffney think about it?"

"Agnes." He gave another gasping little laugh. "High church, you know—but she cooks well."

So Agnes Gaffney was the cook at the Baker house—or very probably anyway. But I wanted to know whom he meant when he said, "It would be funny if she found out."

I put my mouth close to his ear and said quietly, "It would be funny if she did find out."

He frowned. "She'd do something about it—I know her. Sometimes I think she has—I don't like her—I wish she'd go away." His eyes were still closed, and his voice had become fretful.

"Who do you mean?" I whispered tensely. "Tell me who it is, and I'll send her away at once."

But my urgency had got through to him, and he opened his eyes and looked at me suspiciously. "Who are you?"

Vera came bustling into the room before I had time to reply.

"What are you doing in here?" she asked sharply. "You have no right to be here—none whatever. He is not allowed to have visitors."

I said, "Sorry, I got lost," and went out, feeling badly disappointed.

I could hear the voices of Edith and Aunt Isabelle, so I went in there to see what was doing.

The room was lighted, and my aunt was smoking a cigar, while Edith sat in the armchair, trying to keep her eyes open. She gave me a bleary look and said, "Jessie, the night watchman. Terms on request."

It was the sort of so-called humor that exactly suits my aunt Isabelle. She laughed uproariously and told Edith to send it to a radio contest.

I said I was panicked but I was afraid to laugh for fear of bursting my appendix.

Aunt Isabelle turned serious at once. "I'm afraid Michael will insist on removing mine any day now. It's been very troublesome lately."

"Why aren't you two asleep?" I asked, trying not to yawn.

Aunt Isabelle said that youth could hardly be expected to understand or sympathize with insomnia, but Edith answered more practically, "Some noise woke us both. Sounded like something in the old boy's room. I thought he'd fallen out of bed, and I went in to see—but he was all right and there didn't seem to be anything else."

"You'd no right to be asleep anyway," said Aunt Isabelle. "What do you think I pay you for? You'll get fat as a pig, sleeping twenty-four hours out of each day."

I said hastily, "Edith, did you know the cook at the Baker house? I think her name was Agnes Gaffney."

"No kidding," said Edith. "I thought her name was Florence Nightingale.

"A lot you know about Florence Nightingale," said my aunt acidly. "I suppose you think it's a type of bird." She thought that was pretty good and chuckled to herself for some time.

I said to Edith, "The old man said something to me about Agnes being a good cook."

"She must be a whiz," Edith said indifferently. "The old pest used to throw the stuff in their faces."

So Edith didn't know about Agnes Gaffney—and I was afraid to ask the Bakers for fear they'd guess that I had found the will.

"What are you mooning about, girl?" Aunt Isabelle demanded irritably. "If you're sleepy go to bed. In fact, you'd better go to bed anyway."

I said, "Yes, ma'am," and left the room. I walked briskly across the hall, opened and shut my door and then tiptoed back to the chartroom.

Sheila was still there, and William Forrest was talking to her. Vera sat at the desk with her lips folded into a thin line.

Bill appeared, and Forrest left Sheila and joined him. The two of them started down the corridor toward my aunt's room, and I wondered idly what sort of reception they would get. I did not know whether Forrest had made any effort to identify Agnes Gaffney, and I made a mental note to tell him why I thought she must be the Baker cook.

Sheila started chatting with me—mostly about the weather. I asked her why she didn't go back to bed now that they had finished with her room, but she said she wanted to see if they found anything.

Vera went off to answer a light, and I delicately extracted Mr. Baker's address from Sheila. I had no sooner got it than I realized that it was wasted effort—because I could have looked it up in the phone book.

The service elevator droned to a stop, the door opened and the Negro orderly stepped out.

He glanced at us, and I beckoned to him imperiously. He walked over and stood in front of us, his eyes shifting uneasily.

"What have you been doing in the guest suite?" I asked.

Fear showed at once in his dark face and settled any doubt I might have had about him.

"I haven't been in there," he said earnestly. "I'm not supposed—it isn't my place—"

"I know it isn't," I said impatiently in my anxiety to dig the truth out of him. "But you've been there several times just the same. You'll get fired if we tell on you—but we'll keep still if you'll tell us what you were doing in there."

"I never went in the guest suite."

I saw Vera emerge from one of the rooms at the end of the main corridor, and I said quickly, "Here comes the nurse. You have until she gets here to spill it—or else."

He looked up and suddenly a jumble of words poured out, which finally became distinguishable. "Fifty dollars, he said he'd give me if I could find it—and he told me to look in the guest suite."

"Who told you?"

"Mister Baker."

"Which Mr. Baker?"

"That little ole sick Mr. Baker. He told me, you go find it."

"Find what?" I asked breathlessly.

"Black wallet—and—"

"And what?"

"Piece of paper with red writin'!"

CHAPTER THIRTY-SIX

A PIECE OF PAPER with red writing! That was the will—and evidently the old man knew it might have become separated from the wallet.

"Did he say that the paper with red writing was not in the wallet?" I asked sharply.

"No—he said maybe so, maybe not. But he said he'd give me fifty dollars if I found one or the other."

Vera padded up to us and, after giving me a dirty look, sent the orderly on his way.

I followed him down the corridor. "What did you see," I asked, "those nights you were in the guest suite?"

"Nothin'," he declared promptly. "I didn't see nothin' at all."

I let him go. I figured that he probably had not seen anything—and

even if he had he wasn't going to tell me about it. He was obviously
relieved to be rid of me, and he hurried away.

I made a mental note to tell William Forrest that Agnes Gaffney
was probably the cook in the Baker house—and about the orderly lurk-
ing around in the guest suite.

I went back to the chartroom. Vera was writing at the desk, and
Sheila still sat there, staring into space. I offered her a cigarette and
asked her if she had spent the evening in the hospital.

She refused the cigarette and said, "No. I ran home tonight—but
they came after me and brought me back." She stood up abruptly.
"What's the time?"

I glanced up at the clock and said, "Three-thirty."

"I guess I'll go to bed," she said tiredly and went off to the guest
suite.

I looked after her, thinking that the note had been genuine and
wondering whom she had meant by "that black devil." I felt faintly
sorry for her.

"What were you talking to the orderly about?" Vera asked.

"I was trying to make a date with him."

"That may be funny," she said. "I wouldn't know."

William Forrest came back, and I took him to one side and told
him the two things I had kept in mind for him.

He seemed to be interested and said he'd look into them. He went
off after the orderly then and there, and Bill, his assistant, retired to the
guest suite.

I sat down and told Vera, who was scratching away with her pen,
to be quiet, because this was a hospital. She dropped the pen and told
me a lot of interesting and inaccurate things about myself until she had
to go and answer a light that had been on for some time.

I leaned back in the chair and half closed my eyes. I thought I
might go to sleep that way, and if I could it would solve the problem of
finding a safe place to sleep at night from then on.

It didn't work though. Every time I began to drowse off I found
myself sliding off the chair and I came to with a start. I gave it up and
resigned myself to sleeping during the day.

I began to think of Michael and wondered again if he were fond of
me. He had taken Louise out, but I did not know whether he was terribly upset about her death or not. I decided at last that he could not have

been in love with her, because he had joked about her—and going on from there I began to feel pretty despondent, because he joked about me, too—and what went for one case must go for the other.

I had thought in a circle and was back at the beginning. I was about to start all over again when, through my half-open eyes, I caught sight of a nurse peering cautiously around the corner from the stairwell. She was looking at me, and I remained perfectly still and waited. She must have satisfied herself that I was asleep, because she presently emerged, very quietly. She took a swift look up and down the corridor and then came toward me.

I tried to keep surprise from my supposedly sleeping face when I recognized her as the owner of the little perfume bottle. She kept her eyes on me but went past me and disappeared into the guest suite.

I got up at once. I remembered her telling me that she did not know anything about the murders—or that the bodies had been found in the guest suite. I realized, suddenly, that it would be practically impossible for her not to know—the thing must have been all over the hospital like wildfire.

I went into the guest suite and found that it was pitch dark, as usual. I could not see even a white glimmer that might indicate the girl's uniform, so I felt my way to the solarium and turned on the light. She was not there, and after thinking it over for a minute I went back into the hall and to the bedroom I had last occupied there. Bill was sleeping peacefully on one of the beds, so I woke him and told him that there was a stray nurse in the guest suite and he'd better find out what she was up to.

He didn't take to the idea with any enthusiasm.

"There's no one here," he said peevishly. "I can see the door from the bed."

"You mean you sleep with your eyes open?"

He said, "Please, lady," in a voice of long suffering, and added, "I'm supposed to sleep if I want to. All I'm here for is to be on the spot."

"Sure," I said, "it's O.K. I'm always around to wake you if anything happens."

He came with me then and looked through the other bedroom and the solarium. "You bin seein' things," he said disgustedly.

"What about the Baker rooms?"

He said, "Now listen—you gotta be reasonable. I can't wake those people again at this hour."

"No," I admitted reluctantly, "I suppose not."

I went slowly back to the main corridor. Either that nurse had heard me coming and had gone out via the solarium window and the fire escape—or else she was in one of the Baker rooms—and what possible business could she have there?

Vera hailed me and said, "Doctor Rand phoned."

"He what?"

"Phoned," she said irritably. "Telephoned."

"Oh. Why?"

"I don't know why, I'm sure. He said he would be over here in about an hour and he wants you to stay awake until he gets here."

"Was he trying to be funny?" I asked bitterly. "What does he want anyway? Coffee?"

"What were you doing in the guest suite?" said Vera.

I ignored her and walked slowly down the corridor toward my room. Once or twice I looked over my shoulder uneasily. Michael's call sounded ominous somehow—as though he thought I were in danger.

I switched the light on in my room and made a hasty search, but it was empty. I went to the bureau and began to repair my face, but I was nervous and presently dropped the powder puff onto the floor. I stooped to pick it up—and let out a subdued scream. The bed crank was lying on the floor.

CHAPTER THIRTY-SEVEN

IT WAS MEANT for me this time—I was sure of that. I stood there with the puff in my hand, staring at the crank and too terrified for a moment even to move.

I wondered wildly what I had done. I wasn't really mixed up in the thing—I wasn't even a blonde. I had found the will, of course—but then the will had been stolen from me, and I could easily have been killed then. I must have done something since that made it imperative to remove me. But what? I had spoken to the orderly and I had seen the nurse sneak into the guest suite and had followed her.

I looked fearfully around the room and then crept to the door and peered out, but the hall was empty. I decided to make a dash for the chartroom and demand that Bill bodyguard me for the rest of the night.

I eased out the door, and at that moment Edith's head appeared, and she said, "Psst." I went over to her. "The old pest's sleeping," she whispered, "but I can't any more. She woke me up once too often."

"I thought it was a noise from the old man's room that woke you up."

"Hell, no," Edith said disgustedly. "She swore there'd been a noise, so I said it came from the next room to prevent her blaming me."

I said nothing about it to Edith, but I decided, privately, that there probably had been a noise when the two papers were stolen from me.

"Come on with me," I said. "I don't want to stay here."

She said, "Oke," and we walked up the corridor to where Vera sat at the desk.

I asked if Bill were still in the guest suite, and Vera shook her head. "No. He had a telephone message and left."

I could feel the hair rising on my scalp. I was alone, then, and at the mercy of this murderous unknown.

Vera looked at me curiously and asked, "What's the matter with you? Have you seen a ghost?"

"Yes," I said hysterically. "My own."

Edith laughed, and Vera clicked her tongue and said, "What a way to talk."

She had to go then, and I sat down and wondered helplessly what I ought to do. I was glad that Michael was coming, but I didn't expect him for at least half an hour—and killing could be done so quickly.

I glanced at Edith, who was snooping through some charts that didn't concern her, and told her about the nurse who had sneaked into the guest suite. "She belongs on the fifth floor," I said. "Let's go down and see if we can find her, and we'll ask her what she was up to." It had occurred to me that I might be safer on the fifth floor.

Edith agreed, and we went on down. There was a nurse in the chartroom, and she asked us, with a certain amount of reserve, what we wanted. I said we'd come for a visit.

"Whom do you wish to visit?" she asked formally.

I said, "You."

Her eyebrows shot up. "Me?" she asked in great surprise.

"Just a little chat," I said persuasively.

She looked at her watch and then back at us, and I knew, as surely as though she had said it, that she thought I was a nut and Edith was in charge of me.

"It's a little late for a chat," she said soothingly. "Suppose we wait until tomorrow."

I caught sight of the girl for whom we were looking then, and I went after her. She had a hypodermic syringe with a piece of cotton stuck on the end, and when she saw me she nearly dropped it.

I didn't waste any words on her. I asked directly, "What were you doing in the guest suite tonight?"

She blushed, stammered and denied it.

"What's the use of wasting time?" I asked wearily. "I saw you."

After a few more denials she suddenly capitulated, gave her head a little toss and said defiantly, "We love each other."

"You and who else?" I asked, astounded.

"Trevis Baker," she wailed. "But it's a secret. We were not to tell anyone."

"You mean you were not to tell anyone," I said. "Why do you let him get away with stuff like that?"

"It's his uncle," she said indignantly. "He is so unreasonable. He told Trevis he was not to marry a nurse."

"He was kidding," I said. "He's crazy about nurses."

She blinked nervously and said, "I don't know what you mean."

"Did you ever nurse him? The old man, I mean?"

She shook her head. "I never did, and I wouldn't want to."

"Did you see Trevis tonight?"

She blushed and said, with a touch of coyness, "Yes—but he sent me down again just as soon as you had stopped hunting for me." She added hastily, "I only wanted to talk to him, you know."

"I wouldn't care," I said, "if you were on the point of giving birth to twins. But he was angry with you for coming up, wasn't he?"

She nodded miserably.

"Did you see him that other night—when you told me you'd gone up for a nap?"

"No," she said, "I got into the wrong room and I never did find him. But I didn't know it was that dreadful room until you told me."

"You knew Frances had been murdered on the sixth floor though?"

"Yes—I did," she admitted reluctantly. "But you must believe me—I know nothing about those murders—and Trevis doesn't either."

I shrugged and let her go—and Edith sidled up to me. "Did you get anything out of her?"

"Not much," I said indifferently. "She's in love with Trevis."

"So what?" She yawned and added, "Listen, Jessie, I'll have to go back and take a look at your aunt. The old warhorse might have wakened—and I'll be out on a limb."

I went back to the sixth floor with her because I didn't know what else to do with myself. Aunt Isabelle was sleeping loudly, and Edith said, "Let's go into your room and have a cigarette."

I shivered. "Why not go back to the chartroom?"

"I'm not allowed to smoke there."

"All right," I said. "Come on."

As we went across the corridor I distinctly heard someone moving around in Mr. Baker's room.

I was suddenly stiff with fear, but I had not the courage to go back and investigate—even though Edith was with me.

We went into my room and closed the door, and Edith pushed the bureau in front of it. "Better be safe than sorry," she said briefly.

I went to the bureau drawer for cigarettes, and my head was whirling with a kaleidoscope of all the bits and pieces of knowledge that I had gathered together.

Suddenly as I stood there the pieces fell into place, and I knew who the killer was—and at the same instant I looked into the mirror and saw Edith stoop and pick up the bed crank.

CHAPTER THIRTY-EIGHT

I WHIRLED AROUND and heard my voice, high and shrill, saying, "Put that thing down."

She knew that I had guessed—I could see it in her face. Her eyes, hot and vindictive, blazed in her head like coals. "You damnable busybody," she said and threw the crank, with horrifying swiftness and strength.

I twisted sideways, and the thing grazed my shoulder and crashed into the mirror behind me. I screamed and screamed again and began to push frantically at the bureau, while I kept my eyes on her face.

She flew at me, and her hands fastened on my throat. I was helpless against her strength, but I could hear people outside the door, and the bureau began to move crazily into the room.

Darkness, troubled by a confused noise of shouting and shot through with vivid flashes of lightning, gave way to Michael's face, bending over me. I was stretched on the bed, and William Forrest and Bill seemed to be talking to Edith.

Michael said, "My God! Jessie! Didn't you guess?"

"Just about in time," I muttered.

Rather suddenly Edith turned away from the two policemen and flopped into the armchair. She said, "All right—I'll go to your lousy jail."

"No kiddin'?" said Bill. "Gee—thanks!"

Edith flicked him a glance. "Never mind the sarcasm—it was my own filthy temper that tripped me." She hauled out a compact and began to powder her nose. "Stupid people," she said, "always did throw me into a fury." She looked at Forrest. "Want to hear all about it?"

"Love to," Forrest said courteously.

Bill gave his gum a brief rest and stared at them in astonishment.

"I mean it," Edith said slowly, "about my temper having spoiled it all. I'm convinced you'd never have found out otherwise. I realized that Jessie knew—but she couldn't have proved anything. And then I flew into a rage, and you caught me trying to polish her off."

"Why did you want to kill me," I croaked, "if I could not have proved anything?"

"You were getting too damn nosy," she said coldly. "I was afraid you might stumble onto something that would be really dangerous to me—and I thought I'd better finish you before you did."

Forrest murmured politely, "You were about to tell us?"

She settled back into the armchair. "All my life," she said, "I've had nothing—absolutely nothing. I didn't have a beau when all the other girls did—even Vera was able to produce some sort of a crummy specimen—although she couldn't keep him.

"I went to nurse old man Baker, and you can imagine what it meant to me when he suddenly up and told me that I was his sweetheart and he was going to leave me all his money. I couldn't believe it at first, but he took me out to all sorts of expensive places and I was quite thrilled—even though he was old and unattractive. He told me I was his heart interest, and he showed me the will he had made in my favor—and said it was to be kept in a safe-deposit box at the bank.

"All I had to do was to be nice to him and kiss him occasionally. It seemed incredible, and I used to get so excited thinking what I'd do with all that money that I was nearly crazy.

"A couple of months after he showed me the will he suggested that I leave his employ. He said it would be more fun to sneak out and see me. I decided that he was cracked, and I planned to kill him and make it seem like an accident. But I couldn't do it somehow—I couldn't kill the only beau I'd ever had. He had a vile temper—but I didn't mind that. My own is pretty bad—and I rather liked him.

"At his insistence I left and got a job with the Daniel woman. The old cat has never had a day's illness in her life either."

There was a shout from the doorway, and we looked up to find Aunt Isabelle standing there. She started to yell abuse at Edith, but Michael got to her and shut her up.

"This is *one* time when I'm going to have the floor," Edith said, settling her cap. "The old toad can button her lip—or else."

There wasn't a sound out of Aunt Isabelle by way of reply because Michael had his hand firmly over her mouth.

"I didn't care for the Daniel case much," Edith resumed, "but the pay was steady and I got out from time to time. I had only the promise of the Baker money—I hadn't seen the color of it—but he continued to take me out. I tried to get him to take me back on the nursing job, but he wouldn't have it. He said it was more exciting to see me occasionally and that daily contact took the shine off romance. I was fool enough to swallow it.

"After a few others he got Olive Parsons. I wasn't worried about her for nearly a year—until one day, when I had time off, he could not take me out. I was uneasy about it, but it didn't happen again for two months—and then it began to happen frequently.

"I was absolutely frantic. I didn't know what to do—and I took to writing him notes—but he never answered, and the one or two times I managed to see him he declared he'd never received them. About five weeks ago he gave up seeing me altogether.

"I was nearly out of my mind. I was sure he was going to change that will—if he hadn't already done so. I went around to his home, but I was told that he was ill and could see no one.

"At that point dear old Isabelle got one of her attacks of boredom and decided to come to the hospital to relieve it. I had to chaperon her, of course, and the first thing I discovered was that the old man and Olive were already here. I felt swell then. I thought if I could just get a few words with him I'd be able to fix things up.

"I sneaked in at the first opportunity, but to my horror he barely recognized me, and all he would say was, 'Go away, Edith.'

"I went back to my patient, who was in the room formerly occupied by Mr. Baker—she'd had him thrown out and herself installed— and sat down. I felt miserable and depressed and was wondering what to do, when I caught sight of the black wallet, wedged in behind the bureau. I pulled it out and opened it—and got the biggest shock of my life. It contained a few newspaper clippings, one of my own notes, a diamond ring and a new will, leaving everything to Olive Parsons. It had been witnessed by Frances Hoffman.

"I decided to kill them both and keep the will myself."

CHAPTER THIRTY-NINE

"WHAT ABOUT the other witness, Agnes Gaffney?" I asked.

"She's a moron cook," Edith said scornfully. "She doesn't even read the papers. She came after I left, and the old man told me all about her."

There was a moment of silence while Edith stared at the ceiling. "Frances should have told me about that will," she said presently. "She knew about it, and she had a right to tell me. Anyway, I got her—and I got Olive.

"I laughed when I heard about the old man wandering around looking for his wallet. I laughed when I heard of the three younger Bakers looking for it—I had told them what it contained, and they were wild to get their hands on it. And I nearly had hysterics when I heard that Olive was looking for it. I hid it in the toe of old Daniel's shoe.

"I was coming up from my supper, just before twelve on the night I killed Frances, when I saw her disappearing into the guest suite. I followed quietly. The Bakers and Jessie were playing bridge in the solarium, and I saw Frances sneak into Jessie's room. I thought she merely wanted to snoop—there was nothing she liked better. I slipped into the adjoining room, pulled the crank out of the bed and then went into Jessie's room. Frances had her head in the closet, trying to see what sort of clothes Jessie had brought.

"I closed the door quietly and walked up behind her, keeping the crank out of sight—but she was backing out of the closet and hadn't even heard me. I hit her on the back of the head and she fell, and then I finished her off and pushed her under the bed. I replaced the handle in the other room.

"Nobody saw me, and the bridge players had not noticed anything. I went back and took the wallet out of the toe of old Daniel's shoe—if you want to call it a shoe. I took it home with me in the morning. It was just as well, too, because Jessie had caught on to that hiding place.

"Getting Olive was a bit more difficult. I took the crank out of the old man's bed, put it on the floor and waited for an opportunity—but none came. She sat there with her eyes open—and I couldn't risk it. I got mixed up with Jessie in the guest suite, and I pulled one of the cranks out there to have it ready. But apparently Olive replaced the one in Mr. Baker's room, and tidy little Jessie put back the one in the guest suite—so that when my chance did come I had to pull one out in a hurry—and it was the same one that I had used before.

"As a matter of fact, I had given up hope of getting Olive that night. The Baker woman was drunk, and I hung around with her for a while. She never liked me—she called me a black devil—so I always insulted her when I got a chance. Then we found old Daniel, who had disappeared, in Trevis Baker's bathroom—and by the time that was all straightened out I was ready to call it a day. I was just dozing off in the armchair, when I heard Olive leave the old man's room and start up the hall. I went to the door and watched, and to my surprise she walked straight into the guest suite. I hurried after her and found her searching Jessie's room—carefully and without misplacing anything. Jessie was in the solarium with our popular young veterinary, Doctor Rand."

At this point in Edith's narrative Michael dropped his hand from Aunt Isabelle's mouth, and in the interest of all who wished to hear the rest of it, she promptly put her hand over his mouth.

"I watched Olive for a while," Edith went on, "and she suddenly gave up the search and came out into the hall. Luckily the light was out, and it was dark, so that she did not see me. I flattened myself against the wall and saw her go into the other bedroom—where I had killed Frances. I slipped into Jessie's room, pulled out the nearest crank and followed Olive into the next room. It was quite easy. She was looking under one of the pillows—and as she straightened up I let her have it. She went down without a sound, and I made sure of her and then pushed her under the bed. I arranged her so that one leg was showing—just as Frances had been."

Edith sighed and was silent for a moment. William Forrest asked quietly, "What about the other one?"

"Louise," Edith said. "I didn't want to be bothered with her. I had finished what I'd set out to do, and I figured that since I had the will in my possession the earlier one would stand up. I kept that second will next to my skin. I took it out of the wallet and hid the wallet in Daniel's pocketbook. She didn't find it till just a little while before Jessie got it. She hadn't had a chance to look through it so she tried to threaten Jessie by telling her she had found it wrapped up in her green pants. I kept the ring for a while, because I figured that it belonged to me, but later I decided it would be safer out of my possession so I put it on Jessie's bureau. I heard, from Sheila Baker, that she tried to keep it."

The scene changed again then, with both Aunt Isabelle and Michael putting their hands over my mouth.

"Louise came to me," Edith was saying, "and said that Frances had told her about the will. I declared I knew nothing about it, but Louise said it must be around somewhere and that it had been kept in a black wallet.

"I don't know whether she suspected me or notbut I could not chance it. I asked her to meet me in the guest suite and said I'd help her to search—and something about the way she looked at me had me sweating with fear. I went into the guest suite early and pulled out one of the bed cranks.

"She could not get away until quite late, and then she came to Daniel's door and whispered that she'd meet me there. She said nothing more than that, but I had a feeling that she was going to confront me with whatever knowledge she had. I did not want to be seen passing the chartroom, so I told her to go ahead.

"She went on up, and I saw Jessie try to stop her—unsuccessfully. I worked my way up the hall by sliding in and out of the empty rooms. At the last room I got out onto the fire escape and crawled through the small window that gave onto the main corridor. I had to make a dash across the main corridor, and that was my biggest risk—but I was fortunate. Jessie didn't see me, and Vera was nowhere in sight.

"I crawled through the companion window, on the other side of the corridor and onto the other fire escape and climbed in the solarium window.

"Louise was in Jessie's room. She was standing there, looking at the crank, and she was smiling. She did not see me, and I drew back into the dark hall and waited. She started to walk around the room and then, suddenly, she came out into the hall and went into the solarium.

"I picked up the crank in Jessie's room and went quietly to the door of the solarium. Louise had not turned the light on there, and she was standing by the window through which I had come. I think she expected me to come that way. She had stopped smiling and was crying.

"I crept up behind her and saw her stiffen at the last minute—but she never had a chance. After I had finished with her I put her on the chaise longue, closed her eyes and fixed her up to look as though she were sleeping, because I did not want her discovered before I got back to my room. I replaced the handle and got back safely in the same way that I had come.

"Everything was all right until the next evening—last night. I lost the will, and I saw Jessie pick up a piece of paper in the hall. I knew by her attitude that it was important, and I was positive that it was the will.

"I had to wait until she was asleep, in that room across the hall, before I could attempt to get it back. I didn't know where she had hidden it, but she's pretty stupid and fairly obvious, so I tried under her pillow first—and there it was.

"She woke up and touched me as I pulled my hand out, and I had to fly across the hall and arrange myself in the armchair. By the time she came I looked as though I had been sleeping there all night.

"Later I saw her talking to you, Forrest, and I knew she was telling about the will. I was furious and I made up my mind to dispose of her.

She was the only one who had actually seen it—no one else could prove it had ever existed.

"I tagged that redheaded little dumbbell all over the place—and just as I thought I'd caught up with her she saw me in the mirror.

"It was my only failure—and I blame myself. I should have kept my temper and bided my time."

CHAPTER FORTY

Michael and I had to help Aunt Isabelle back to bed. She looked really ill, for the first time in her life.

Vera looked in at us, her eyes as big as saucers, but Aunt Isabelle saw her and told me to shut the door. Vera took offense and went off, and my aunt said, "Only to think—all those years—and that creature breaking bread with me day after day."

"I've been very uneasy for some time," Michael said slowly. "I've hung around the place most of the night, but last night I had to go out of the county on a case and just before I started home I thought of something. I'd seen Edith lose her temper once at your home, Miss Daniel. She did not know I was watching, and it was some trivial thing—I believe one of the maids stepped on her toe. She flew at the girl in a fury and beat her about the head. I hadn't thought of it again until last night—and then it made me so uneasy that I telephoned and came straight here."

"I never thought of suspecting her," Aunt Isabelle said feebly.

I glanced at Michael and said, "It came to me just before she attacked me. You see, I found the will in our corridor—and no one was using it except Vera, Edith and Trevis at that time. The Gregg Bakers were not visiting just then. It could not have been on the floor for long, so I figured it had to be one of those three.

"I was pretty sure that Trevis had never had it in his possession—the three of them were still searching and obviously worried. Vera seemed too stupid for such intrigue, and anyway, she has a tremendous pride in her own virtue. She could never have done all that and kept it off her face and out of her speech.

"But Edith was different. I knew she was an accomplished liar—she told you a few hot ones, Aunt Isabelle."

My aunt snorted. "I never believed one of them," she said. "Never paid any attention to her."

"Be that as it may," I said tactfully, "after I had settled on Edith as the person who had lost the will I realized that she must be attempting, in some way, to get Mr. Baker's money for herself. She had killed the three girls already for it—and at that point I saw her pick up the handle and start after me."

"You ought to be more careful," Aunt Isabelle said, reaching for a cigar. "Letting a woman like that nearly brain you."

"I wonder who searched the vacant room next to mine in the guest suite the first night I was there," I said, looking at Michael.

"It must have been Olive," he said promptly. "The old man probably told her that the will was missing, and she was worried. I suppose she was afraid he'd die before she found it, and she made a pretty extensive search. She must have known that Edith was out gunning for it—if she didn't already have it."

"Then who was moving about Mr. Baker's room when Edith and I came in here?" I asked.

"Vera," said Michael. "She was standing just outside the door when I came down the corridor."

Aunt Isabelle yawned and flicked ash from her cigar. "I think you ought to X-ray my appendix," she said to Michael.

"You ought to thank him for hanging around when he thought you were in danger," I suggested. "Or maybe it was his fifty thousand."

"What's this?" said Aunt Isabelle.

"Nothing," said Michael. "Feeble attempt at sarcasm."

"What fifty thousand is the girl talking about?"

"The fifty thousand," I said, "that you were going to give him for taking me off your hands. If I had been killed he wouldn't have got it."

Michael lit one of Aunt Isabelle's cigars and made faces at me through the smoke.

"Nothing of the sort," my aunt barked. "Utter rubbish. I never offered him fifty thousand at any time. I promised to settle that sum on you—but I meant you to keep it to yourself and for yourself."

I looked at Michael and asked simply, "Why the lie?"

"Oh hell," he said, throwing the cigar out of the window. "I had to have some excuse to admit that I was going to marry you."

"What's all this nonsense?" said Aunt Isabelle. "What are you talking about? And I'll thank you, Michael, not to waste my good cigars."

I stood up. "I hope," I said coldly, "that all our children have bright red hair."

Aunt Isabelle roared with laughter.

THE END

Rue Morgue Press Titles as of August 2000

The Black Stocking by Constance & Gwenyth Little. Irene Hastings, who can't decide which of her two fiances she should marry, is looking forward to a nice vacation, and everything would have been just fine had not her mousy friend Ann asked to be dropped off at an insane asylum so she could visit her sister. When the sister escapes, just about everyone, including a handsome young doctor, mistakes Irene for the runaway loony, and she is put up at an isolated private hospital under house arrest, pending final identification. Only there's not a bed to be had in the hospital. One of the staff is already sleeping in a tent on the grounds, so it's decided that Irene is to share a bedroom with young Dr. Ross Munster, much to the consternation of both parties. On the other hand, Irene's much-married mother Elise, an Auntie Mame type who rushes to her rescue, figures that the young doctor has son-in-law written all over him. She also figures there's plenty of room in that bedroom for herself as well. In the meantime, Irene runs into a headless nurse, a corpse that won't stay put, an empty coffin, a missing will, and a mysterious black stocking. As Elise would say, "Mong Dew!" First published in 1946.   **0-915230-30-5 $14.00**

The Black-Headed Pins by Constance & Gwenyth Little. "...a zany, fun-loving puzzler spun by the sisters Little—it's celluloid screwball comedy printed on paper. The charm of this book lies in the lively banter between characters and the breakneck pace of the story."—Diane Plumley, *Dastardly Deeds.* "For a strong example of their work, try (this) very funny and inventive 1938 novel of a dysfunctional family Christmas." Jon L. Breen, *Ellery Queen's Mystery Magazine.*   **0-915230-25-9 $14.00**

The Black Gloves by Constance & Gwenyth Little. "I'm relishing every madcap moment."—*Murder Most Cozy.* Welcome to the Vickers estate near East Orange, New Jersey, where the middle class is destroying the neighborhood, erecting their horrid little cottages, playing on the Vickers tennis court, and generally disrupting the comfortable life of Hammond Vickers no end. Why does there also have to be a corpse in the cellar? First published in 1939.   **0-915230-20-8 $14.00**

The Black Honeymoon by Constance & Gwenyth Little. Can you murder someone with feathers? If you don't believe feathers are lethal, then you probably haven't read a Little mystery. No, Uncle Richard wasn't tickled to death—though we can't make the same guarantee for readers—but the hyper-allergic rich man did manage to sneeze himself into the hereafter. First published in 1944.   **0-915230-21-6 $14.00**

Great Black Kanba by Constance & Gwenyth Little. "If you love train mysteries as much as I do, hop on the Trans-Australia Railway in *Great Black Kanba,* a fast and funny 1944 novel by the talented (Littles)."—Jon L. Breen, *Ellery Queen's Mystery Magazine.* "I have decided to add *Kanba* to my favorite mysteries of all time list!...a zany ride I'll definitely take again and again."—Diane Plumley in the Murder Ink newsletter. When a young American woman wakes up on an Australian train with a bump on her head and no memory, she suddenly finds out that she's engaged to two different men and the chief suspect in a murder case. It all adds up to some delightful mischief—call it Cornell Woolrich on laughing gas.   **0-915230-22-4 $14.00**

The Grey Mist Murders by Constance & Gwenyth Little. Who—or what—is the mysterious figure that emerges from the grey mist to strike down several passengers on the final leg of a round-the-world sea voyage? Is it the same shadowy entity that persists in leaving three matches outside Lady Marsh's cabin every morning? And why does one flimsy negligee seem to pop up at every turn? When Carla Bray first heard things go bump in the night, she hardly expected to find a corpse in the adjoining cabin. Nor did she expect to find herself the chief suspect in the murders. This 1938 effort was the Littles' first book.   **0-915230-26-7 $14.00**

Brief Candles by Manning Coles. From Topper to Aunt Dimity, mystery readers have embraced the cozy ghost story. Four of the best were written by Manning Coles, the creator of the witty Tommy Hambledon spy novels. First published in 1954, *Brief Candles* is likely to produce more laughs than chills as a young couple vacationing in France run into two gentlemen with decidedly old-world manners. What they don't know is that James and Charles Latimer are ancestors of theirs who shuffled off this mortal coil some 80 years earlier when, emboldened by strong drink and with only a pet monkey and an aged waiter as allies, the two made a valiant, foolish and quite fatal attempt to halt a German advance during the Franco-Prussian War of 1870. Now these two ectoplasmic gentlemen and their spectral pet monkey Ulysses have been summoned from their unmarked graves because their visiting relatives are in serious trouble. But before they can solve the younger Latimers' problems, the three benevolent spirits light brief candles of insanity for a tipsy policeman, a recalcitrant banker, a convocation of English ghostbusters, and a card-playing rogue who's wanted for murder. "As felicitously foolish as a collaboration of (P.G.) Wodehouse and Thorne Smith."— Anthony Boucher. "For those who like something out of the ordinary. Lighthearted, very funny.'—*The Sunday Times*. "A gay, most readable story."—*The Daily Telegraph*.   **0-915230-24-0**   **$14.00**

Happy Returns by Manning Coles. The ghostly Latimers and their pet spectral monkey Ulysses return from the grave when Uncle Quentin finds himself in need of their help—it seems the old boy is being pursued by an old flame who won't take no for an answer in her quest to get him to the altar. Along the way, our courteous and honest spooks thwart a couple of bank robbers, unleash a bevy of circus animals on an unsuspecting French town, help out the odd person or two and even "solve" a murder—with the help of the victim. The laughs start practically from the first page and don't stop until Ulysses slides down the bannister, glass of wine in hand, to drink a toast to returning old friends.   **0-915230-31-3**   **$14.00**

Come and Go by Manning Coles. Young Richard Scorby thought he could escape his domineering Aunt Angela and her attempts to marry him off to the girl of her choice by running away to Paris. Only Richard didn't count on his aunt's determination to see him married or the determination of certain crooks—whose last job he had witnessed— to see him dead. Fortunately, Richard has a couple of guardian angels in the form of two long-dead cousins, James and Charles Latimer, who are able to return from the dead whenever a relative is in a spot of trouble. Accompanied by their claret-loving pet monkey Ulysses, these two gentlemanly ghosts appear and disappear across Paris and the French countryside before finally managing to set this earthly world straight. It all adds up to a comic gem, much what you would have gotten had P.G. Wodehouse added ghosts to a Bertie Wooster/Jeeves novel.   **0-915230-34-8**   **$14.00**

The Chinese Chop by Juanita Sheridan. The postwar housing crunch finds Janice Cameron, newly arrived in New York City from Hawaii, without a place to live until she answers an ad for a roommate. It turns out the advertiser is an acquaintance from Hawaii, Lily Wu, whom critic Anthony Boucher (for whom Bouchercon, the World Mystery Convention, is named) described as "the exquisitely blended product of Eastern and Western cultures" and the only female sleuth that he "was devotedly in love with," citing "that odd mixture of respect for her professional skills and delight in her personal charms." First published in 1949, this ground-breaking book was the first of four to feature Lily and be told by her Watson, Janice, a first-time novelist. No sooner do Lily and Janice move into a rooming house in Washington Square than a corpse is found in the basement. In Lily Wu, Sheridan created one of the most believable—and memorable—female sleuths of her day.   **0-915230-32-1**   **$14.00**

Death on Milestone Buttress by Glyn Carr. Abercrombie ("Filthy") Lewker was looking forward to a fortnight of climbing in Wales after a grueling season touring England with his Shakespearean company. Young Hilary Bourne thought the fresh air would be a pleasant change from her dreary job at the bank, as well as a chance to renew her acquaintance with a certain young scientist. Neither one expected this bucolic outing to turn deadly but when one of their party is killed in an apparent accident during what should have been an easy climb on the Milestone Buttress, Filthy and Hilary turn detective. Nearly every member of the climbing party had reason to hate the victim but each one also had an alibi for the time of the murder. Working as a team, Filthy and Hilary retrace the route of the fatal climb before returning to their lodgings where, in the grand tradition of Nero Wolfe, Filthy confronts the suspects and points his finger at the only person who could have committed the crime. Filled with climbing details sure to appeal to both expert climbers and armchair mountaineers alike, *Death on Milestone Buttress* was published in England in 1951, the first of fifteen detective novels in which Abercrombie Lewker outwitted murderers on peaks scattered around the globe, from Wales to Switzerland to the Himalayas.

0-915230-29-1 $14.00

Murder is a Collector's Item by Elizabeth Dean. "(It) froths over with the same effervescent humor as the best Hepburn-Grant films."—Sujata Massey. "Completely enjoyable."—*New York Times.* "Fast and funny."—*The New Yorker.* Twenty-six-year-old Emma Marsh isn't much at spelling or geography and perhaps she butchers the odd literary quotation or two, but she's a keen judge of character and more than able to hold her own when it comes to selling antiques or solving murders. Originally published in 1939, *Murder is a Collector's Item* was the first of three books featuring Emma. Smoothly written and sparkling with dry, sophisticated humor, this milestone combines an intriguing puzzle with an entertaining portrait of a self-possessed young woman on her own in Boston toward the end of the Great Depression.

0-915230-19-4 $14.00

Murder is a Serious Business by Elizabeth Dean. It's 1940 and the Thirsty Thirties are over but you couldn't tell it by the gang at J. Graham Antiques, where clerk Emma Marsh, her would-be criminologist boyfriend Hank, and boss Jeff Graham trade barbs in between shots of scotch when they aren't bothered by the rare customer. Trouble starts when Emma and crew head for a weekend at Amos Currier's country estate to inventory the man's antiques collection. It isn't long before the bodies start falling and once again Emma is forced to turn sleuth in order to prove that her boss isn't a killer. "Judging from (this book) it's too bad she didn't write a few more."—Mary Ann Steel, *I Love a Mystery.*   0-915230-28-3 $14.95

Murder, Chop Chop by James Norman. "The book has the butter-wouldn't-melt-in-his-mouth cool of Rick in *Casablanca.*"—*The Rocky Mountain News.* "Amuses the reader no end."—*Mystery News.* "This long out-of-print masterpiece is intricately plotted, full of eccentric characters and very humorous indeed. Highly recommended."—*Mysteries by Mail.* Meet Gimiendo Hernandez Quinto, a gigantic Mexican who once rode with Pancho Villa and who now trains *guerrilleros* for the Nationalist Chinese government when he isn't solving murders. At his side is a beautiful Eurasian known as Mountain of Virtue, a woman as dangerous to men as she is irresistible. Together they look into the murder of Abe Harrow, an ambulance driver who appears to have died at three different times. There's also a cipher or two to crack, a train with a mind of its own, and Chiang Kai-shek's false teeth, which have gone mysteriously missing. First published in 1942.   0-915230-16-X $13.00

Death at The Dog by Joanna Cannan. "Worthy of being discussed in the same breath with an Agatha Christie or Josephine Tey...anyone who enjoys Golden Age mysteries will surely enjoy this one."—Sally Fellows, *Mystery News.* "Skilled writing and brilliant characterization."—*Times of London.* "An excellent English rural tale."—Jacques

Barzun & Wendell Hertig Taylor in *A Catalogue of Crime*. Set in late 1939 during the first anxious months of World War II, *Death at The Dog*, which was first published in 1941, is a wonderful example of the classic English detective novel that first flourished between the two World Wars. Set in a picturesque village filled with thatched-roof-cottages, eccentric villagers and genial pubs, it's as well-plotted as a Christie, with clues abundantly and fairly planted, and as deftly written as the best of the books by either Sayers or Marsh, filled with quotable lines and perceptive observations on the human condition. **0-915230-23-2 $14.00**

They Rang Up the Police by Joanna Cannan. "Just delightful."—*Sleuth of Baker Street* Pick-of-the-Month. "A brilliantly plotted mystery...splendid character study...don't miss this one, folks. It's a keeper."—Sally Fellows, *Mystery News*. When Delia Cathcart and Major Willoughby disappear from their quiet English village one Saturday morning in July 1937, it looks like a simple case of a frustrated spinster running off for a bit of fun with a straying husband. But as the hours turn into days, Inspector Guy Northeast begins to suspect that she may have been the victim of foul play. Never published in the United States, *They Rang Up the Police* appeared in England in 1939. **0-915230-27-5 $14.00**

Cook Up a Crime by Charlotte Murray Russell. "Perhaps the mother of today's 'cozy' mystery . . . amateur sleuth Jane has a personality guaranteed to entertain the most demanding reader."—Andy Plonka, *The Mystery Reader*. "Some wonderful old time recipes...highly recommended."—*Mysteries by Mail*. Meet Jane Amanda Edwards, a self-styled "full-fashioned" spinster who complains she hasn't looked at herself in a full-length mirror since Helen Hokinson started drawing for *The New Yorker*. But you can always count on Jane to look into other people's affairs, especially when there's a juicy murder case to investigate. In this 1951 title Jane goes searching for recipes (included between chapters) for a cookbook project and finds a body instead. And once again her lily-of-the-field brother Arthur goes looking for love, finds strong drink, and is eventually discovered clutching the murder weapon. **0-915230-18-6 $13.00**

The Man from Tibet by Clyde B. Clason. Locked inside the Tibetan Room of his Chicago luxury apartment, the rich antiquarian was overheard repeating a forbidden occult chant under the watchful eyes of Buddhist gods. When the doors were opened it appeared that he had succumbed to a heart attack. But the elderly Roman historian and sometime amateur sleuth Theocritus Lucius Westborough is convinced that Adam Merriweather's death was anything but natural and that the weapon was an eighth century Tibetan manuscript. If it's murder, who could have done it, and how? Suspects abound. There's Tsongpun Bonbo, the gentle Tibetan lama from whom the manuscript was originally stolen; Chang, Merriweather's scholarly Tibetan secretary who had fled a Himalayan monastery; Merriweather's son Vincent, who disliked his father and stood to inherit a fortune; Dr. Jed Merriweather, the dead man's brother, who came to Chicago to beg for funds to continue his archaeological digs in Asia; Dr. Walters, the dead man's physician, who guarded a secret; and Janice Shelton, his young ward, who found herself being pushed by Merriweather into marrying his son. How the murder was accomplished has earned praise from such impossible crime connoisseurs as Robert C.S. Adey, who cited Clason's "highly original and practical locked-room murder method." **0-915230-17-8 $14.00**

The Mirror by Marlys Millhiser. "Completely enjoyable."—*Library Journal*. "A great deal of fun."—*Publishers Weekly*. How could you not be intrigued, as one reviewer pointed out, by a novel in which "you find the main character marrying her own grandfather and giving birth to her own mother?" Such is the situation in Marlys Millhiser's classic novel (a Mystery Guild selection originally published by Putnam in 1978) of two women who end up living each other's lives after they look into an antique Chinese mirror. Twenty-year-old Shay Garrett is not aware that she's pregnant and is having second thoughts about marrying Marek Weir when she's suddenly transported back 78 years in time into the body of Brandy McCabe, her own grandmother, who is unwillingly about to be married off to miner Corbin Strock. Shay's in shock but she still recognizes that the picture of her grandfather that hangs in the family home doesn't resemble her husband-to-be. But marry Corbin she does and off she goes to the high mining town of Nederland, where this thoroughly modern young woman has to learn to cope with such things as wood cooking stoves and—to her—old-fashioned attitudes about sex. In the meantime, Brandy McCabe is finding it even harder to cope with life in the Boulder, Co., of 1978.   **0-915230-15-1 $14.95**

About The Rue Morgue Press

The Rue Morgue Press vintage mystery line is designed to bring back into print those books that were favorites of readers between the turn of the century and the 1960s. The editors welcome suggestions for reprints. To receive our catalog or make suggestions, write The Rue Morgue Press, P.O. Box 4119, Boulder, Colorado 80306. (1-800-699-6214).